THE BLACKSTONE LION

ALSO BY ALICIA MONTGOMERY

THE TRUE MATES SERIES

Fated Mates

Blood Moon

Romancing the Alpha

Witch's Mate

Taming the Beast

Tempted by the Wolf

THE LONE WOLF DEFENDERS SERIES

Killian's Secret

Loving Quinn

All for Connor

THE BLACKSTONE MOUNTAIN SERIES

The Blackstone Dragon Heir

The Blackstone Bad Dragon

The Blackstone Bear

The Blackstone Wolf

The Blackstone Lion

ABOUT THE AUTHOR

Alicia Montgomery has always dreamed of becoming a romance novel writer. She started writing down her stories in now long-forgotten diaries and notebooks, never thinking that her dream would come true. After taking the well-worn path to a stable career, she is now plunging into the world of self-publishing.

facebook.com/aliciamontgomeryauthor

twitter.com/amontromance

bookbub.com/authors/alicia-montgomery

To Mom,

I know sometimes I say stupid things and do stupid things, especially when I was younger.
But I want you to know, I'll always be your baby girl
And you'll always be my mom.

I love you.

THE BLACKSTONE LION

BLACKSTONE MOUNTAIN BOOK 5

ALICIA MONTGOMERY

PROLOGUE

THIS WAS NOT how Luke Lennox thought his day would go.

He certainly didn't expect to start it by confronting an entire biker gang and then end it with a suicide rescue mission with no backup.

Dr. Violet Robichaux didn't seem like it, but she could be one crazy chick. Barging into the old canning factory guarded by armed men only proved it.

"Fuck." He clenched his fists at his sides. "Let's go before she gets herself killed." He had barely finished his sentence before Nathan, Violet's mate, disappeared through the doorway.

"Damn women," he muttered as he barged into the laboratory. Why was it even the most reasonable shifter males lost their fucking minds when it came to their mates? The notorious womanizer Nathan Caldwell was no different. *I don't even know why I give a fuck.*

Nathan's nose was probably sensitive enough to know where Violet had gone, so Luke followed the wolf shifter until they reached one of the rooms inside the factory.

"Don't you ever do that again," Nathan said through gritted teeth as he approached his mate.

"It's her," Violet gasped. "Joanne."

Luke came closer, glancing at the frail girl on the bed in the middle of the canning room turned lab. This was the girl they had risked their lives for. His inner lion raged, seeing her state. She was dressed in a white paper gown with wires sticking out of her. Her face was the color of ash and her lips cracked and dry.

Just when he thought humankind's cruelty had reached its lowest, they go and do something like this. *Those fucking assholes*. He looked around the room. It was as sterile as the rest of the facility, with various types of medical equipment all around. There were several beds, but only two were occupied—Joanne and another girl. As they had suspected, the factory had been turned into some kind of laboratory that experimented on shifters.

"Is she okay?" Violet asked as Nathan checked on the other girl.

"Heartbeat's faint, but she seems to be hanging in there."

There was no time to lose. Gently, Luke picked up Joanne. The scent of feathers tickled his nose. *Flight shifter*. Glancing over at Nathan, he saw that he was lifting the other girl off the bed.

Luke nodded to the door. "Let's get them out of here."

Violet's face was serene as she nodded in agreement, but he knew the animal she kept reined in was roaring to get out. Just like his lion.

The sooner they were out of here, the better. He'd never admit it out loud, but this place gave him the creeps.

They were only one step out of the lab when the alarms went off. Luke knew things would only get harder from here.

Nathan cursed. "Shit! They know we're here."

"Had to happen eventually." Luke cocked his head toward the exit. "C'mon. We need to get out in case they have lockdown procedures."

"Someone's down there." Violet pointed down the opposite end of the hallway. "She needs our help."

"We'll come back for her! Let's go now and save these two," Nathan insisted.

Thank God someone around here was thinking straight.

"No! I'm not leaving anyone behind!" Violet began to walk away from them.

"Goddammit!" Nathan turned to Luke and handed him the girl in his arms. "Get them out of here!"

Luke easily slung the second girl over his right shoulder as he tucked Joanne under his left arm. He gave Nathan an affirmative grunt as he pivoted and headed toward the door. Behind him, he could hear the pounding of boots and the sounds of clothes ripping as Violet and Nathan shifted into their animals.

Damn fools. They already had two girls. Why the hell were they risking their lives to save one more? The equation didn't make sense, but he didn't have time to think about it now.

Luke made it to the exit without incident, which solidified his earlier suspicions. This place wasn't well-protected. Its best defense was keeping a low profile. The factory had been abandoned for decades and no one passed by the old highway anymore. Which is probably why those bastards used it to conduct their experiments.

Thinking about what they might have done to these girls or any shifter made his blood rage in his veins. But there would be time for that later. Right now, he had to get these girls to safety.

Luke walked around to the front. It was empty, though there was a garage. When he entered the rickety structure, he saw the nondescript Honda sedan inside.

Jackpot. It was even unlocked and the keys were in the ignition. These people really didn't expect to be discovered.

Luke placed the two girls in the back seat and shut the door. He was about to get into the driver's side when he stopped, his hand frozen at the latch.

There it was again. The sound of a woman's voice. He had heard it earlier, before Violet lost her shit and re-enacted her solo version of D-Day on the place. He had initially ignored the way it made the hairs on his arms stand on end, but now, he just *couldn't.*

His lion roared, urging him to go back.

"We gotta go," he said in a gruff voice. But the animal ignored him. Damn lion loved a fight. It helped feed the blood thirst that always seemed to be bubbling just under the surface.

"Fine." He let go of the car door and strode outside, marching back toward the facility with purposeful strides. As he went inside, he saw two more guards running down the hallway, toward the door where Nathan and Violet had headed earlier. *Fuck.* As he shucked his jeans down, he let out a whistle, catching the guards' attention.

The two goons turned on their heels. They were so surprised at the fully-grown lion jumping toward them, they didn't even have time to raise their guns. He pounced on them, knocking one back so he slammed against the wall, while the other ended up beneath him. The lion let out a roar before swiping a paw that slashed down the man's face.

"No!"

The sound of her voice was tugging at something deep in

his chest. The lion took over and charged toward the sound, sprinting as fast as he could to the door at the end.

"You stupid whore!" someone shouted.

As Luke sailed through the door, he saw a tall man in green scrubs stagger forward. The woman he had clutched to his chest broke free, but the man's arms swung wildly. Luke saw something glinting in his hand that made adrenaline pound through his veins even faster. Instinct told him he couldn't let the man harm her.

He lunged at the man, using his claws to scratch down his back, which elicited a scream. Luke had never seen him before, but in his gut he knew this man was responsible for the suffering of many shifters. He didn't even think twice as he opened his mouth and sank his teeth into his head.

When the man stopped moving and struggling, he released the lifeless skull from his jaws. The lion stepped back and began to shift.

As he transformed back into his human self, Luke grabbed a rag from a table and wiped the blood from his mouth and chest. It would be a long time before he'd feel clean again, but it was worth it, knowing the evil bastard was dead. Was he the leader of this shadowy group that was hell-bent on killing every shifter in the world?

Luke threw the rag aside and glanced at the bloody mess on the floor. Someone as important as the head of an underground operation like this probably wouldn't have been this vulnerable or easy to kill. His instincts were telling him there was someone higher up the chain.

The distinct clang of claws hitting metal caught his attention. Glancing to the side, he saw Nathan standing by a stack of cages. The scent of various furs, feathers, and scales hung in the air, and Luke realized what those cages were for.

I'm going to tear all of them apart, then hunt down the bastards who did this. He strode toward Nathan, who had unlocked the cage with his claws. The other cages seemed to be empty, but—

Luke felt like he had hit an invisible brick wall. As his eyes landed on the woman next to Nathan, his heart stopped, only to speed back up at an alarming rate.

Mine! His lion roared.

He was so stunned, he hardly noticed the small figure who clung to her.

"Mommy," the little blond boy said in a hoarse voice. "The bad man ... is he gone?"

"He won't hurt you anymore."

The growl escaped his lips before he could stop it. It must have been loud enough because it startled Nathan.

"Luke, you okay, man?"

Mine!

His lion's unearthly voice was the only thing he could hear aside from the roaring of his blood in his ears. Every muscle in his body tensed up. *It couldn't be. She couldn't be—*It took every ounce of his strength, but he managed to tear his gaze away from her and turn around.

"Luke! Where are you going?"

A muscle spasmed in his jaw. "Outside."

"Outside?"

"Yeah." There was a thickness coating his throat that he didn't even realize was there. Clearing it, he simply said, "Jason and Christina will be here any minute," before walking away.

His lion fought him with each step that took him farther away from her. *We can't,* he told his inner animal. *We're not meant for a mate. This isn't right.*

His words were answered by angry growls.

"No!" he roared. *We can't have her. Besides, she's already got a man.*

Ugly jealousy reared its head, but he pushed it down. He didn't have the chance to look at her for long, but her image was burned into his mind. Plump, pink lips. Long, silky hair like a mahogany waterfall. Large brown eyes. A softly-rounded face. She was obviously distraught, but he could imagine her with a big smile that would reach those doe-eyes. Looking up with a sweet expression, not at him, but her husband, the father of her bear cub.

She could never be his. There had to be some mistake. He knew his lion was fucked up, so it probably got its wires crossed.

"Luke!"

He spied the familiar Range Rover parked next to the garage. Jason and Christina had finally arrived.

"What happened?" the dragon shifter asked.

"It's a long story but," he nodded at the factory, "Nathan and Dr. Robichaux are still in there. They're going to need your help."

"We're on it," Jason said. "Where are you going?"

"We found more kidnap victims," he explained. "I got them safe, but I should bring them to the hospital."

"Good idea." Jason clapped him on the shoulder. "You okay, man?"

"Yeah. Why?"

Jason shrugged. "I dunno. You just look a little … disturbed."

Luke huffed. "If you went in there, you'd know why."

"Are Nathan and Violet okay?" Christina asked.

"They should be out soon." Without further explanation,

he marched toward the garage, to the girls he left behind in the car.

The breathing of the two girls sounded normal enough, so he knew they'd be okay until they reached Blackstone Hospital's ER. Verona Mills was closer, but they'd be much better off in Blackstone than at some human-run place.

Forget about her, he thought as he turned the key in the ignition. He gripped the wheel tight and gnashed his teeth. She and her cub are safe, and soon, they'll be on their way home. That was all that mattered.

CHAPTER ONE

THIS WAS NOT how Georgina Mills thought her life would turn out.

Her sheltered upbringing didn't prepare her for this. For anything that happened in the last five years of her life. It was a total one-eighty.

Still, looking at Grayson and his sweet face as he smashed another piece of apple pie into his mouth, Georgina wouldn't trade him for the world. She shuddered to think what would happen if her life had taken the trajectory it was supposed to. The life she had been groomed for.

She shook her head mentally. The past was the past, and it was done. Grayson was her life now. Taking care of him was her priority. That old life was gone. And good riddance.

"Georgina, are you okay?" Catherine Lennox's pretty face was marred with concern, her clear blue eyes staring right at her. "You seem a million miles away."

Something like that. Georgina swallowed. "I'm just … you know … thinking."

"Oh, dear." Catherine put an arm around her. "I was

hoping it wasn't too soon for you to be out and about since, since ... you know."

Had it only been a week ago that she and Grayson had been rescued from Dr. Mendle's laboratory? She gave Catherine a tight smile. "It's fine. I mean," she glanced at Grayson, who was now on his third slice of pie, "I'm glad we can go out and Grayson can experience some normalcy."

They were at Rosie's Bakery and Cafe, where it seemed half the town had gathered for Nathan and Violet's going away party. The two of them were leaving this evening to build orphanages in some remote country in the Caucasus. The couple was standing in the middle of the room, laughing and chatting with a group of their friends. They were the ones who came in and rescued her and Grayson, so she was sad to see them go, but knew they were needed elsewhere.

Catherine put a hand over hers. "Whenever you're ready. I'm here if you want to talk more."

"Thank you." She had already given her rescuers the short version of what happened. They'd been living in Wyoming when they were kidnapped by Dr. Mendle and his men. They locked up Grayson and made her do menial tasks in the lab. But she didn't offer them any other information.

Catherine, Matthew, and everyone involved in their rescue assumed that Dr. Mendle kidnapped Grayson because he was a bear shifter. Their assumption was partly right, but Georgina didn't bother to tell them the whole story. It didn't matter anyway. Because if they did find out—

"Georgina, lovely to see you."

The posh, polite tone startled her, and Georgina found herself looking up at a familiar face. "Hello, Christina." It still unnerved her a bit to be in the same room as Christina Lennox. Not just because she and Catherine were identical twins, but also because her frosty blue eyes seemed to see *everything*. It was like she could tell Georgina was hiding something.

Christina sat down on the opposite side of Grayson. "Hello, Grayson. How are you? Are you enjoying the pie?"

Grayson mumbled something through a mouthful of pastry.

"Grayson!" Georgina admonished. "Don't talk with your mouth full."

The little boy swallowed the rest of his pie and then let out a loud burp. "I'm fine, Miss Christina. And the pies here are delicious!"

Georgina felt mortified, but Christina chuckled and ruffled his hair. "I'm glad you like it."

"Can I have one more, Mommy?" Grayson asked.

"Grayson, you have to leave some for the others," Georgina said.

Catherine laughed. "Don't worry, there's plenty of pie. I think Nathan and Violet bought out Rosie's supplies for the day."

"Please, Mommy? I'm still hungry!"

A pain pricked at her heart. Grayson barely had an appetite while they were in the lab. Though Dr. Mendle hadn't put him through any of the sick experiments he conducted on the other shifters, he often threatened the boy to control *her*. To keep her in line and punish her. It was, of course, on the orders of The Chief. Just saying that name in her mind made her skin crawl.

"Well, if you're hungry, go ahead and grab another slice from the table." He stood up, but before he could run off, she stopped him. "Just one, okay? And you *will* eat all your veggies tonight, young man."

He nodded. "I promise, Mommy."

"Okay, go and get your pie."

"Oh boy!" Grayson zoomed off to the table, his eyes growing large as Rosie set another tray of fresh pies down.

"He's precious," Catherine said, the look on her face wistful. Georgina didn't fail to notice that look; the other woman often had it when she was around Grayson.

"Don't worry," Christina said, obviously knowing what her twin was thinking. "It'll happen for you guys."

"We've been trying for months," she said. "I just … I don't know …."

"It's harder for dragon shifters," Christina said.

"They aren't as fertile as bears or wolves," Georgina added. "That's why you don't see many of them just flying around."

Christina's gaze flickered at Georgina, her eyes narrowing.

"That's what I heard, anyway," she added quickly.

Catherine sighed. "Riva did mention that. It took months before she got pregnant with Jason and Matthew. And years before they even had Sybil. And they wanted more, but just couldn't."

"So tell me, Georgina," Christina began. "Grayson's what, four or five years old?"

"Just turned five," she said.

"So you were pretty young when you had him?"

She nodded and gave a nervous laugh. "Yeah. Nineteen. Too young to know any better, I'm afraid. He was a surprise but not unwanted." Oh no. She loved Grayson fiercely, from the moment she knew he existed. That was the same moment her entire world changed.

"Did they perform any experiments on him? Was there a reason Dr. Mendle wanted a bear cub when he mostly kidnapped adult shifters?"

"Christina!" Catherine exclaimed. "This is not the time."

"I—Sorry, Georgina." Christina let out a frustrated sigh. "I'm just curious."

Georgina felt the blood drain from her face, and she stood up. "It's getting really stuffy in here. If you'll excuse me, I need air." She pushed her chair back, stood up, and headed to the exit, leaving the sounds of laughter and merriment behind her as she walked out the door.

Surely Christina didn't suspect anything. Why would she? She wasn't from the local police or the feds. Or maybe … Georgina swallowed the lump in her throat. They were judging her. Thinking it was her fault they'd been kidnapped. And well, they were right. But better for them to think she was a bad mother than to find out the *whole* truth.

The tinkling of the bells that signified the door to the cafe had opened made her whip her head around. Catherine emerged and when she spotted Georgina, walked up to her.

"Georgina," Catherine said. "Sorry about that. Christina tends to rub some people the wrong way."

"No worries."

"It's still too soon for you, I told her."

Georgina's brows furrowed. "Too soon for what?"

"Huh? Um, nothing." She grabbed Georgina's arm. "We should head back inside. The party's winding down and Nathan and Violet will be leaving soon."

"All right."

She followed Catherine inside, her eyes instinctively scanning the room for Grayson. She saw him seated at their table, Christina beside him as he ate his pie. Perhaps she was being paranoid, but she couldn't afford to let her guard down, even for a second. She had been careful back in Wyoming, and yet, The Chief managed to track her down and have them kidnapped as she was picking Grayson up from his babysitter.

"Attention, attention!" Nathan whistled, and the room quieted down. He was standing in the middle of the room with Violet right beside him. "So, first of all, I just wanted to say thank you to everyone who showed up. Wow, I thought a couple of people would celebrate me getting out of town, but not all of you." Everyone laughed. "Seriously though, I never thought I would want to leave Blackstone. Ma and Pop made the right decision coming here, that's for sure. We were welcomed with open arms, even when the rest of the world shunned us." A hush fell over the room. "This was the place I grew up and where my family is. Kate," he turned to the young woman to his left, "you take care of yourself, okay?"

Kate tossed her dark blonde and pink locks. "Like I couldn't do that. You're still leaving me the Mustang, right?"

Nathan laughed. "Yes. Now, Matthew, Jason, Ben, we may not be related, but you're like my brothers. I mean, you *are* my brothers." He smiled fondly at the three men who were standing together off to the side. "Even Luke, that bastard." He chuckled. "He knocked on my door last night to say goodbye."

"Very late last night," Violet said with an annoyed snort and a roll of her eyes.

He pulled Violet closer to his side. "I can't say it enough, but thank you for everything. I can't call what we have friendship, because it goes much deeper than that. And thank you for your understanding. I want you to know that even though I'm leaving, you guys call if you need me and I'll be there. My heart belongs to my mate, but Blackstone will always have a special place in it."

Violet smiled warmly at Nathan. "It's special to both of us, love."

Matthew stepped forward. "We're sad to see your ugly mug go, man, but you know you're always welcome to come back anytime."

"I know," he said, giving him a grateful smile. "Well, it's almost that time."

More well-wishers and guests came forward to give their goodbyes to the happy couple. Georgina sat in the corner with Grayson, trying to stay out of everyone's way as they crowded around the happy couple. However, right before they left, Violet and Nathan came over to her and Grayson to say goodbye.

"What are you going to do now?" Violet asked.

Good question. "I'm not really sure."

"You should stay in Blackstone," Nathan said. "This place is special. Grayson can go to school, find some friends like him. I think he'd be really happy here."

"I'll have to think about it." Did she want Grayson to grow up around caring, loving people? Around his own kind? Of course she did. She cast an envious glance at Violet and Nathan, and all the happy couples around her. Living in Blackstone seemed like a fairy tale. But she was no princess in this story.

Perhaps cementing the fact that this place was even more fairy-tale like was the magnificent Blackstone Castle. It was the home of the Lennox dragons, or in this case, just one—Matthew Lennox—and his wife and mate, Catherine.

After Georgina and Grayson had been rescued and checked out at the hospital, Jason had taken them to the castle. To say she was impressed was an understatement. Blackstone

Castle was huge and intimidating, with its tall spires, towers, and imposing presence. Even Grayson, who had been exhausted by the entire ordeal, suddenly woke up and got excited when he saw the place.

"This is the safest place in Blackstone," Jason had explained. "And Matthew and Catherine would be happy to have you stay."

So they'd been staying here as guests for the past few days. Catherine and Matthew had welcomed them warmly and gave them a huge bedroom for their own use. That first night, Georgina could hardly keep from tearing up as it was the first time she'd held Grayson in weeks, since he spent all his time locked in that cage. He clung to her so tight, she could hardly breathe, but she didn't dare pull away. It was as if she were afraid it would all be a dream and she'd wake up to another nightmarish day.

"It's still early for supper," Catherine said as they entered the castle. After Nathan and Violet left, they all piled into Matthew's car and headed back home. "Why don't we go exploring first?"

"Oh, can we?" Grayson asked, his big brown eyes lighting up.

"Well, I suppose—"

"Yay!"

Matthew leaned down and kissed his wife's cheek. "I have work to do in my office. I'll see you all at dinner." He headed toward his private office, and Georgina, Catherine, and Grayson walked the opposite direction, to the eastern part of the castle.

"As I've mentioned before," Catherine began. "On the second floor of the west wing are Riva and Hank's private apartments. They had the castle re-done so that the entire east wing belongs to the kids. They each have their separate apartments with the connecting common rooms, plus there's the guest bedroom where you guys are staying."

"It's bigger than I originally thought," Georgina said. "Is it very old?"

"Hmmm ... let me see if I remember what Christopher told me the first time I came here," she said, mentioning the Lennox's butler. "It was built by Lucas Lennox, that's Matthew's great-great-great-great-grandfather and the first Blackstone dragon. He won the mountains in a card game and decided to come here. He discovered the blackstone deposits, built the mines, and became one of the richest men in America."

"Cool!" Grayson said. "So he used all that money to build a castle?"

"Not at first," Catherine said. "He built the town first, envisioning it as a place where all shifters could live together in peace. Most shifters live in groups, for safety reasons. If you noticed, there's no real pack, den, or clan here, but rather, they all kind of live under the protection of the Blackstone dragons. They welcome all kinds of shifters."

"So Matthew's kind of the Alpha around here?" Georgina asked.

"Unofficially, I guess," she said with a laugh. "More like a protector. I mean, Hank is still alive, and he's technically the more senior dragon, and then there's Jason and Sybil. Anyway, so apparently, Lucas Lennox fell in love with a beautiful Swedish countess while he was in Europe. He wanted to marry her and take her back to America, but she said she'd only do it if he built her a castle. And so he did."

"Eww!" Grayson stuck his tongue out. "He made this cool castle ... for a girl?"

Catherine chuckled. "I guess he's at that age where he thinks all girls are gross."

"They are! Except Mommy," Grayson clarified. "And you too, Miss Catherine."

"Thank you, Grayson," she said as she patted Grayson on the head and then led them into one of the rooms. "This is the family room," Catherine explained. "It's one of the more modern parts of the castle. Riva had everything refurbished sometime after she married Hank. Most of the public areas and the outside grounds have been preserved, but she wanted everyone to feel comfortable in the private rooms."

The family room did indeed look cozy. There was a large, leather sectional sofa in the middle with a lot of pillows and warm throws, a huge flat screen TV that took up an entire wall, and a fireplace in the corner.

"Woohoo!" Grayson dashed for the sofa and immediately started jumping on it.

"Gray—"

Catherine placed a reassuring hand on her arm before she could continue. "Don't worry about it," she said with a laugh. "That's what it's there for. That sofa was strong enough to withstand four shifter kids growing up here. I'm sure Grayson won't even scratch it."

Four? Georgina thought maybe she heard wrong.

"Mommy! Mommy! Look at me!" Grayson leapt forward to dive into the cushions, but he somehow lost control and knocked over a large picture frame that was on the console table behind the couch.

"Grayson!" Georgina rushed to her son. "Be careful!"

"I'm sorry, Mommy!" Grayson's lower lip trembled.

"Shhh … it's okay," Catherine said, planting herself beside

the little boy. She picked up the frame. "Nothing here is breakable." She tapped the photo. "Plastic and wood."

"Let me put that back," Georgina said with a sigh as she took the frame from Catherine. As she put it back on the table, she froze and stared at the picture inside.

She recognized three of the young teens in the photo—the identical smiles of Matthew and Jason, plus the only girl in the picture, Sybil, the youngest of the Lennoxes. All of them shared the same dark hair and silvery gray eyes. However, the fourth person in the photo didn't resemble any of them. Even though he was probably no older than fifteen, he was half a foot taller than the twins. His long blond hair went down to his shoulders and his serious expression wasn't similar at all to any of the three.

"Who's that?" It sounded rude, but she couldn't help herself.

"Who?" Catherine asked, then scrunched her eyes at the photo. "Oh. You mean Luke?"

"Is that his name? Who is he?"

"You don't know him?" Catherine's brows were drawn together in confusion. "He was there at the canning factory. When you guys were rescued."

"There wasn't any—" A gasp escaped her mouth. *The lion.* The one that killed Dr. Mendle. "I thought I was hallucinating. I saw him … but …."

The memory was blurry, like a fuzzy dream. But suddenly it became clear as day: the tawny gold eyes of the lion. And the fierceness of the animal as it devoured Dr. Mendle. Georgina stared back at the photo. Those were definitely the same eyes. "That's him. Is he a family friend or something?"

"He's adopted," Catherine began. "According to Matthew, they found Luke as a cub, when he had wandered into the castle grounds. He was in bad shape and barely conscious. When he woke up, he couldn't remember anything—where he was from, who his parents or pride were, or even his name or what happened to him. Riva and Hank eventually adopted him and raised him along with their kids."

"Huh." She brushed a finger on the photo. "Does he live here? How come I've never seen him?"

"Umm," Catherine cleared her throat, "Luke prefers to be alone. He's not really close to his family."

"Why?" Everyone in Blackstone was so nice, plus the Lennox children all seemed so warm and welcoming.

"It's not really my place to tell you," Catherine said. "I'm sorry."

"It's fine. I just …." She glanced over to the other photos on the table. There were a couple more of the kids, all arranged in chronological order it seemed—baby photos, family vacations all over the world, portraits as they reached grade school age, sports photos as they were in their teens, high school and college graduation photos, and some of them as adults at various functions. Georgina noticed that Luke didn't make an appearance in the later pictures. The last one of him was the photo Grayson had knocked down.

"He's been estranged from them for a while," Catherine explained, as if reading her mind.

"You don't have to say any more." Those golden eyes stared back at her, as if boring into her soul. She rubbed her arms, feeling the gooseflesh that appeared over her skin.

She didn't want to think about it anymore, even though there was an ache in her heart that seemingly appeared from nowhere. There was no use feeling anything from a man she had never met and probably never would.

"Grayson, sweetheart, I think I see some books over there."

She pointed to the shelf in the far corner. "Maybe Miss Catherine will let us borrow one for bedtime tonight?"

"Go ahead," Catherine said. "Pick as many as you want."

"Thank you!" Grayson said, already halfway to the shelf.

"Catherine," Georgina said in a low voice. Hopefully Grayson would be distracted enough he wouldn't try to listen in. "I wanted to talk to you about something."

"What is it?"

"Yes, well, er," Georgina took a deep breath, "I want to thank you, for your generosity. You didn't even know us and you welcomed us. Gave us food and clothes and—"

"Shush." Catherine squeezed her shoulder. "It's nothing at all. You know, I was in a similar situation once."

"Really?"

Catherine nodded. "Yeah. I kind of ran away from home. It's a long story, but in the past, people have shown me a lot of kindness, too. Especially here in Blackstone. So this is a chance for me to pay it forward."

"That's very nice of you," she said. "But my point is, we can't stay here forever, sponging off you and Matthew."

"Oh, it's not—"

"I know you guys are, like, rich as Midas," Georgina chuckled, "but still. I'm an adult and a mom. I need to provide for my son and be a good example."

"Oh." Catherine fidgeted in her seat. "What would you do, though? Go back to Wyoming?"

Georgina bit her lip. It wouldn't be safe. Surely, The Chief would be keeping a watch at her old work and apartment. Besides, there was nothing to go back to. She had no home, no savings, not even a car to take them away. Was there a word that meant worse than dire? Because whatever it was, that's what she was in now. But she would find a way.

"I suppose I could get a job. I was a receptionist at a vet's clinic for four years. Before we were, uh, taken."

Catherine's eyes lit up. "That's it! Matthew and Jason don't have an assistant."

"They don't?"

"No. Their mom and dad, who were CEO of Lennox Corp. and president of the Lennox Foundation, shared an assistant, Martha Caldwell. That's Nathan and Kate's mom. She retired along with Riva and Hank and all their friends. I could ask Matthew if he'd be willing to take you on."

"Really?" Her heart soared, but she kept a hold on her emotions. "I mean, only if he thinks I'm qualified."

"I'm sure you'll do fine," Catherine said. "I'll tell him over dinner. And you guys can work it out."

"That would be great. I'll work any job, really," she said. "Thank you."

"You're welcome. Now, let's help Grayson pick something out before he takes the entire shelf down."

Grayson had all the books within his reach scattered on the floor. But Georgina couldn't bring herself to scold him, not when he looked so happy. Besides, this was the start of a plan. Work, save and scrimp every cent, and then leave Blackstone. Everyone here had been so wonderful, and they were all good and kind people. They wouldn't deserve what Georgina would be bringing down on them if The Chief found out they were protecting her and her son.

CHAPTER TWO

THE LION WAS silent as it padded through the thicket of trees. Keen feline eyes cut through the darkness, seeing everything. It moved forward, lithe and graceful, not making a sound. It knew every inch of the forest; every tree, rock, and bush were burned in its memory. Stalking the territory, scouting out danger. Keeping everyone safe. It had been doing this since it was a cub.

Growing up, Luke knew he was different. Hank and Riva had never kept the fact that he was adopted a secret. How could they? But it wasn't just because he was a lion and they were dragons.

No. His lion was different. He couldn't control his animal. It was so dominant that it scared other shifter kids away. Hank was the only one who could manage him. He taught Luke how to tame his lion though it wasn't nearly enough. Most shifters, given proper instruction, were able to take hold of their animal sides. Something was wrong with him and as he grew older, he was slowly losing control. He was worried he was going crazy and that meant one thing: if he went feral, he would have to be put down.

And that's when Hank suggested expending his energies elsewhere. If he couldn't get any sleep because his lion was bothering him, he should let it roam. And so, with Hank's supervision, he went out in the evenings in lion form. Hank accompanied him every night until he knew the land like the back of his hand, then let him roam on his own. The lion relished the freedom, staking its claim on the territory, watching out for danger and keeping it away. His animal needed an anchor, a purpose, and it somehow found it, doing these nightly patrols.

Blackstone Castle loomed in the distance, and the lion pushed forward. The moon wasn't that high up in the night sky yet. Tonight's patrol started early, as it had the past few days. Not that the lion minded. It didn't sleep anyway. Couldn't sleep. Not when danger was everywhere.

Must keep everyone safe, Luke said from inside his lion's body. Nothing too unusual to report in the last quadrant. He really should move east from here and finish that section of his map. But it was like his paws had a life of their own, bringing him closer to the castle.

Where the hell are you going?

But that was a rhetorical question, of course. Luke knew where it was going. To the same place.

The lion walked over to the large spruce tree, pushing on its hind legs and leaping up the trunk as his claws sank into the wood. Swiftly and silently, it crept up the ancient tree, climbing the branches higher and higher until it reached the canopy up top. This particular spruce was so big and so old, it reached halfway up the length of the castle. And, from where the lion perched on its most outward branch, Luke had the perfect view inside.

Not just anywhere inside, but into the guest room. And, as was her custom this time of night, *she* was sitting by the window, looking up at the sky.

Mine.

Try as he might, Luke ignored his lion's proclamations. But he knew it would do no good. The lion witnessed every single one of his friends fall for their mates. They were all good men, who deserved the love and happiness a mate could give them.

But he wasn't one of them.

Denying his lion would only cause trouble, but Luke was determined to stay away from her. His human part, anyway. She had never met him or laid eyes on him, so she probably never felt the pull that brought fated mates together. It would be better this way, especially if she had a husband or lover waiting for her. Her cub's father.

Where the hell was he? Why didn't Christina and Jason track him down yet? If she and the cub were his, he wouldn't—

But they weren't his. So he should just stop those thoughts.

Something must have caught Georgina's attention because she turned her head toward the room and smiled. She moved aside, and the boy came up beside her and gazed out the window.

Mine.

She's not, Luke admonished. *And she'll never be.*

She pointed up to the stars, her mouth moving, as if explaining something to him. He nodded along, moving his gaze from her to the heavens and then back to his mother again. The adoration in his face was evident, and he looked at her as if she were the most important thing in the world.

A different kind of emotion pricked at him. It was an even more dangerous thought, and he quickly quashed it. The past was the past. He'd made his bed, and now he had to lie in it.

The boy spoke, and she nodded, then gave him a kiss on the forehead before he bounded off. She remained by the window, turning her head in Luke's direction. For a second, he thought she'd caught him. But he was too far away, and she was human; no way she could see him in the dark.

Her lips parted, and her eyes remained fixed in his direction. Luke didn't make a sound or any movement. She shuddered visibly and rubbed her hands on her bare arms as if she felt a chill. With an intake of breath, she stepped back and closed the curtains.

This is the last time, he told his lion. She'll be gone soon. Because, surely, she had her life to go back to. One where she lived in a perfect home, with her perfect husband, and her perfect child. He had to stay away from her and make sure their paths would never cross again.

Luke parked his truck in the visitor's section of the lot at Lennox Corp. As soon as he entered the complex, Jenkins, the kind old man who had been the guard at the gate since Luke was a teen, waved him in. He pointed Luke to the executive parking garage, but he went the opposite way instead. He was pretty sure the managers and VPs wouldn't appreciate seeing his busted up old Ford truck next to their Lexuses and BMWs.

He turned the engine off, slipped out of the driver's seat, and walked across the lot where he entered the glass and steel building that was the Lennox Corp. Headquarters.

"Good morning Mr. Lennox." The bright-eyed receptionist

stood up from her table to greet him. "On your way to the executive suite?"

He grunted in an affirmative.

She flashed him a smile that was all straight white teeth. "I'll buzz you right in, Mr. Lennox. The elevator's waiting."

Even as he walked away, he could feel the receptionist's eyes on him. He wasn't stupid; he had seen the appreciative look in her eyes. Her heartbeat had sped up when he approached and the slight flush on her cheeks and neck indicated her arousal. Women seemed to find him attractive, but he didn't care one way or the other. During the past few years, the lure of an attractive woman seemed less and less appealing.

The elevator dinged, signaling its arrival. He entered and pressed the button for the top floor, mentally preparing for his meeting with Jason and Christina. Things were getting serious now, and they had to find out who was trying to harm them, before they struck again.

Luke walked toward the familiar office of the CEO of Lennox Corp. and the President of Lennox Foundation, the titles that had been held by Riva and Hank Lennox and now by their twin sons. When the building was renovated and expanded, they had their offices built right next to each other. Even during work hours, the two had been inseparable. And when they retired, it was only natural for their sons to take over. Sybil, on the other hand, went her own way, preferring to work as a social worker. He was so proud of her, his Sybbie, for forging her own path and following her heart.

Riva had tried to give him some type of position at Lennox, which he scoffed at. No, he wasn't the suit and tie type; he preferred working in the mines. The physical work kept his animal steady, and the money wasn't bad. He didn't need much to survive anyway.

As he came closer to the waiting area outside the executive offices, he froze. There was an unfamiliar scent in the air—heady and delicious, like apples and cinnamon. There was also a familiar figure sitting on the chair that used to be occupied by Martha Caldwell. She was staring at the computer screen, her brows drawn together in concentration.

Even though his brain was telling his feet to turn around and get the fuck out, his body remained rooted in its spot.

Mine, his lion purred.

It had been days since he'd seen her. Like he promised himself, that was the last night he went to the castle. It stuck, but he wasn't expecting to run into her anywhere else, much less outside Jason and Matthew's offices.

He wasn't sure how long he was standing there. Certainly, long enough for her to notice. She whipped her head up from the computer screen. Soft brown doe eyes went wide with shock, and a small sigh escaped her plump pink lips.

"It's him," she said in a voice so soft a normal human wouldn't have heard it. She stood up and walked over to him, her heels padding across the plush carpeted floor. "Hi. You're Luke, right?" Her voice made something in his gut ache.

How the hell does she know my name? "What are you doing here?" he asked.

His words must have come out rougher than he'd intended because she flinched. "I-I-I work here," she stammered. "I'm Jason and Matthew's new assistant. Well, trying to be." She laughed, a sound that reminded him of tinkling bells. "It's my first day."

"Hey, Georgina?" Matthew's head popped out from behind his door. "Could you come in here for a sec?" His silvery gaze fixed on Luke. "Oh, hey Luke. You here to see Christina and Jason?"

He cleared his throat. "Yeah."

"Sit tight then. They're downstairs on the 15th floor, but they should be back any sec. Georgina?"

"Oh right. Sorry, Matthew." She straightened her shoulders and pivoted on her heel. Luke stared after her, watching her walk away from him and disappear into Matthew's office without a backward glance.

She works here? Now he was really confused. Why would she be working at Lennox? Where was her husband? He huffed and then sat down on the leather couch. He glanced at Jason's door and then at the elevator. Maybe he should just go down and meet them at the fifteenth floor.

A small sound caught his attention. He frowned and turned toward the source. Two small hands clutching the side of the table. A small reddish-blond head peeked out from under the desk. A pair of eyes blinked at him.

The head disappeared when he realized Luke was staring right back at him. A few seconds later, the boy came crawling out from underneath the desk. He instantly recognized him. Georgina's cub.

"Are you supposed to be here?" he asked.

"I'm 'sposed to be with Miss Irene," he said in a quiet voice. "But ... my bear wasn't ready. It tried to come out and play with the other kids. They have a no-shifting rule."

He grunted. Many of Lennox's employees took advantage of the on-site daycare the company provided. If the boy's bear wasn't used to being around other young, it could have been excited.

The boy walked closer, his brown eyes peering up at him. Luke could tell the bear cub inside him was wary now, as if assessing his animal. To his surprise, his normally dominant lion went still, not wanting to scare the cub away.

He gave Luke a lopsided grin. "I'm Grayson," he said, sticking his hand out.

Luke stared down at the tiny hand.

"My mommy says gentlemen always introduce themselves and shake hands when they meet someone."

Unsure what else to do, he took the small hand, engulfing it with his own. "I'm Luke."

"Nice to meet ya, Mr. Luke," he said with a gap-toothed smile, his neck craning back so he could look up at him.

"It's just Luke," he corrected.

"Grayson?"

Luke and Grayson both turned their heads toward the sound of his mother's voice.

She walked toward them, the expression on her face tight, and bent down to his level. "Grayson, honey, why don't you go back and play at my desk."

"Okay, Mommy." He looked up at Luke. "Nice to meet you, Luke." He scampered off, disappearing under the desk.

"I'm sorry," she said. "Was he bothering you?"

"No."

"We haven't been introduced," she said. "I'm Georgina. Georgina Mills."

"Luke," he said. Like her son, she held her hand out. He hesitated for a moment but took it. Her palm was soft and warm, and standing this close to her, her sweet scent was even stronger. He also didn't fail to notice the blush on her skin and her heartbeat speeding up as their hands touched. It made him quickly pull away.

"You were there. When Nathan and Violet came to the lab. And you ... Dr. Mendle ...."

"That sick bastard is gone." The lab had been burned to the ground, probably by the same people who ran it. Jason had said they didn't find any bodies or evidence the lab had even ever existed. "He won't hurt you and your boy anymore."

"I-I-I just wanted to say thanks." She choked up. "For saving us. I haven't had a chance to say it."

"No need."

"Is there any other way I can say thank you? How about dinner? I'm a decent cook, though I don't have a kitchen. Not even my own place," she said, biting her lip. "I could cook you dinner. At your house."

His lion let out a roar of pleasure, thinking of its mate in their den. He shut that thought down quickly. "Where's your man?"

"Huh?" Her delicate dark brows drew together.

"Your cub's father."

"Oh." Her breath became shaky. "He doesn't have one. I mean he does, obviously. Did. But Grayson's father passed away before he was born."

He stared at her, dumbfounded.

"Luke, sorry about the wait, man."

Luke had been so distracted, he didn't hear the elevator or the sound of Jason and Christina walking up to them. "No big deal," he answered.

"Hello, Luke," Christina greeted. "Thanks for coming. We have a lot to talk about."

"Let's go into my office," Jason said. "Georgina, no calls, okay?"

"Sure thing, Jason." Georgina glanced at Luke, but said nothing, then quickly scampered to her desk. His gaze followed her, like she was prey on the savannah.

"Luke?" Jason waved a hand in his face.

He snapped his head back. "Let's go." He followed them into the office, doing his best to ignore Georgina's presence as they walked by her. His mind was still reeling from her offer and he realized he didn't get to answer her question. Not that he would ever say yes. Today had been a fluke; had he known she'd be here, he never would have come. It was too risky. Her attraction to him was obvious, and his damn lion had picked up on it.

Mi—

"Why is she here?" he asked Jason in a gruff voice as soon as the door slammed shut behind them.

"Who? Georgina?" Jason walked around to his desk and sat in the chair. Christina sat down in one of the seats in front of the large oak desk that had belonged to Hank Lennox. "We hired her to be our assistant."

"Why?"

"Why?" Jason frowned. "Because we need one and she has the experience."

"But why *her?*"

"Is there something the matter, Luke?" Christina's cool blue eyes perused him. "What's wrong with Georgina?"

"She needed a job, and she has a kid to provide for," Jason said.

"And it was the perfect way to keep her here," Christina added.

"Keep her here?" Luke gripped the arm of the chair so tight, he could hear the wood crack under his fingers. With a deep breath, he relaxed and let go.

"We can't let her leave," Christina said. "Not until she tells us what she knows about The Organization."

"The Organization?"

"That's what we're calling them for now," Jason said.

"Those people out to get us. Since they don't seem to have a name."

Luke huffed. "So, why can't you let her leave? You think she's lying?"

"I know she's not telling us the whole truth," Christina said. "I can feel it."

Luke could tell right when she arrived in Blackstone that Jason's mate was much smarter than she let on. She may not be a shifter, but she had finely honed instincts like one. "What do you think she's hiding?"

Christina shrugged. "I don't know."

Or, maybe, Christina didn't want to tell Luke.

"Anyway, there's a reason we called you here, man," Jason said.

"And what's that?"

"Remember the burned-out canning factory?"

"Yeah."

Christina's lips curled into a smile. "Not everything was lost. We found something important. A game-changer."

"What is it?"

"The Organization thought they'd gotten rid of everything in that fire," Jason said. "But we combed every inch of it and found Dr. Mendle's personal diaries and computer."

"He was so paranoid, he kept them in a hidden compartment under the flooring of his lab," Christina added. "Our people back in The Agency are looking at them as we speak." The Shifter Protection Agency was a secret organization Christina's adoptive father and Alpha of the Lykos pack, Aristotle Stavros, had established to counteract anti-shifter activity all over the world.

"Did they find anything?"

"A lot. Too much," Christina said. "They're still sifting

through everything. It's going to take weeks to organize and catalogue everything, especially the handwritten diaries. We found over two dozen notebooks. He must have started writing in them years ago, then switched to using his laptop. The doctor kept meticulous notes and diaries of his experiments and his dealings with The Chief."

"That's the leader of The Organization, as far as we can tell. Dr. Mendle was pretty high up in the leadership structure, but he wasn't the big boss. Mendle most likely ran the science and medical department."

"You have information on the experiments he performed?"

"Yes," Jason said, his jaw setting into a hard line. "Or we will."

"And any of their past dealings." There was a quiver in Christina's voice that Luke had never heard before. He knew the whole story, of course; that Ari Stavros had established The Agency because his mate, Christina and Catherine's mother, had been murdered by The Organization.

"So, what can I do?"

"Keep your up nightly patrols," Christina said. "You've done a great job so far."

He nodded. It wasn't like he had anything else to do. "I'll keep my eyes peeled. But we can't let these bastards—"

"We won't be sitting around, waiting for them to strike," Jason said, his silvery eyes glowing with an inhuman light.

"We have to be careful," Christina warned. "They can't know that we know about them. According to Nathan and Violet, Dr. Mendle said The Organization's influence is everywhere. They even go as far as bribing the local police force in towns to hide any evidence of crimes."

"That's why they got away with kidnapping those shifters in Verona Mills," Jason said.

"For now, we need to gather more information," Christina continued. "We're nearly ready to start operations of the Blackstone arm of The Agency. We're using the fifteenth floor of the building as our headquarters. We're telling everyone it's going to be a new research agency that Stavros International and Lennox Corp. are starting. A couple of our guys will be here soon. Our main liaison from Lykos is supervising the move of the staff, then he'll be coming to Blackstone to be part of the team."

Hiding in plain sight. Luke had to admit it was a good idea.

"Once we have everything set up, we'll be concentrating on finding The Organization," Christina continued.

"But, when we do find them, we won't be twiddling our thumbs." Jason stood up and crossed his arms over his chest. "We need to know you'll be with us. When the time comes."

"You don't even have to ask." He wanted to get these assholes, too. For what they tried to do. For all the things they'd done.

"Good. We're keeping things quiet," Jason said. "Only dad, Matthew, Ari, and now you know all the details."

They chatted for a few more minutes, with Luke reporting on the findings from his nightly patrols. When they were done, Luke stood up. "I'll see myself out. And contact you for anything else."

Luke left Jason's office, his mind still on what Jason and Christina had told him. He was so preoccupied he didn't realize Georgina was standing right in his way and he nearly ran into her.

She let out a soft shriek and toppled back. He reached out to steady her, pulling her close to his body. Her hands landing on his chest were the only thing that prevented her from pressing up fully against him. Still, she was near enough he could smell her scent. And notice her soft, luscious body. She wasn't wearing her suit jacket and there was a hint of cleavage peeking through the top of her blouse.

Wide eyes looked up at him, and a blush spread across her cheeks. She took a step away from him. "Sorry, I was calling your name and you didn't hear me. I didn't want to miss you again." The redness deepened. "Not that I miss you ... or anything."

"It's fine." He turned to leave, but a hand on his bicep stopped him. "Was there something else?"

"I ..." She bit her lip. "So how about that thank-you dinner?"

"For what?"

"Like I said, for saving me and Grayson. I could bring him. Or not." Her eyes went even wider, nearly engulfing her face. "I mean, I don't know if your house is child proofed. But he's a good kid and—"

"Anyone who was there would have done the same. Nathan and Violet did most of the rescuing anyway. I was just tagging along to keep them out of trouble."

"Right."

"So, no need for thanks." He turned away from her.

"Well, okay then. Bye ...."

The disappointment in her voice was clear, even to him. His lion roared with disapproval, urging him to go back. *Mine.*

Abso-fucking-lutely not. This whole mate thing would end right here. He couldn't get involved, even if she was free. She and her cub didn't need someone like him, who was fucked up and came with a boatload of baggage. No, from now on, he would keep his distance, until she forgot all about him. And maybe someday, he too could forget about her.

CHAPTER THREE

"Mommy, Mommy, look what I made!"

Georgina looked down at Grayson, who was holding up a sheet of paper in front of his face. "Wow, sweetie, that's great!"

"It's us, Mommy!" He pointed at the two figures in the middle of the drawing. It was a stick figure woman with brown hair holding the hand of a small bear cub. He drew a big red heart around it.

"You're turning into a great artist," she cooed. "Now, let me finish getting ready, okay? Auntie Kate's gonna be here soon. Why don't you draw a picture for her?"

"Okay, Mommy." Grayson rushed out of her room.

Georgina looked at herself in the mirror for the 136th time that night and sighed. Her hair was freshly washed and blow-dried, her face made up, and the orange dress she wore was cute, despite not being expensive.

It wasn't that she didn't find herself attractive, but she knew she wasn't a beauty. Her eyes were too big, her hair was a mousy color, and her body ... she didn't even want to think about that. She'd always been a little chunky growing up and being pregnant hadn't helped. Her ass and hips were too large, her tummy too flabby. At least she had decent boobs.

"Why do I even bother?"

Maybe because her ego had suffered a huge blow and even now, it made her cringe, thinking about what had happened. What had gotten into her, inviting herself to a man's house to cook him dinner? A man she had just met. Luke Lennox was so obviously not interested in her. Even though it was weeks ago, the memory of that morning at the office made her wince again.

"Gahh!" She kicked her legs. Even now, the humiliation felt fresh. But she couldn't blame him. He was single, handsome, and *sexy as H-E-double hockey sticks*. Why would he want a woman with baggage?

"Grrr!" She sat up and crossed her arms over her chest. Grayson was not baggage. He was her son and the most important thing to her. If a man couldn't accept that, then she had no time for him. Even if he was six-and-a-half-feet of deliciousness that she wanted to lick like a lollipop.

"*Stop.*"

She couldn't let her libido get the best of her. After all, she was getting her life together, and she was once again standing on her own two feet and providing for Grayson.

It had been nearly a month since she started working at Lennox Corp. The salary Matthew and Jason had offered her seemed way too generous, but they warned her that she would be working hard, so she accepted it.

And they weren't kidding. Keeping up with their schedules and appointments was difficult at first, but she had found her stride. The work could be grueling some days, but it felt good to be doing honest work and taking home a paycheck.

They even managed to find a home to rent and moved in

last weekend. It's not that she wasn't grateful to Matthew and Catherine, but Blackstone Castle didn't feel like home. She had been willing to swallow her pride as long as she could, as the deposit on an apartment would take her a couple of months to save, but she couldn't wait to have her own space.

It was a stroke of pure luck that she was having lunch with some workmates at the Lennox Corp. cafeteria when she was introduced to Wendy from accounting. Wendy was moaning about how her asshole landlord wouldn't let her out of her lease and she couldn't move in with her new fiancé. She was looking for someone to take over the remaining nine months of her contract. Georgina jumped on the opportunity without a second thought.

Wendy was only happy to sublet her cute two-bedroom house at the edge of town. She even let Georgina keep the deposit with the landlord, and pay her back in installments, plus babysitting Wendy's seven-year-old daughter every other week so she and her fiancé could have date nights.

With the money she saved, Georgina was even able to get a decent second-hand car to bring her and Grayson to work every day. He still wasn't able to join the other kids at the daycare, and she was only glad her bosses were nice enough to let him stay in the executive suites until he was ready or she could find other arrangements for childcare. Really, everyone in Blackstone had been kind to her. She would miss them a lot when she and Grayson had to leave.

The sound of the doorbell knocked her out of her thoughts, and Georgina got up from the bed. Smoothing her dress down, she was determined to at least have some fun while she could and forget about Luke Lennox. She grabbed her purse and headed to the living room.

"Georgina!" Kate greeted when she opened the door. She

was wearing a scandalously short black tube dress and high heels. Her long, dark blonde hair with pink tips was curled in waves around her shoulders, and her nose piercing sparkled as she moved her head to inspect Georgina. "Looking good, hot momma!"

"Thanks, Kate." The she-wolf shifter had taken it upon herself to take Georgina under her wing, helping her with everything from getting Internet set up at her house to helping her bring her car to J.D., one of the best mechanics in town, for an inspection. Tonight was Kate's birthday and she was having a party at The Den. Though Georgina wasn't into going out to bars, it was difficult to say no.

"Auntie Kate! Auntie Kate!" Grayson was running at full speed, barreling into Kate's legs.

"Oh, hey Grayson!" She bent down and hugged the little boy.

Grayson held up a piece of paper. "I drawed this for you, Auntie Kate. Happy birthday." She insisted Grayson call her that, instead of 'Miss Kate,' because it made her feel like, as she said, "the spinster aunt in some gothic horror romance novel."

Kate held up the drawing and smiled. "That's very cool, Grayson. Thanks." It was a drawing of a wolf with brown and pink hair and a sparkly nose piercing, standing on its hind legs. "You and Penny and Ben will have a great time coloring and playing and doing all kinds of fun stuff at their cabin."

"Go and get your things, Grayson," Georgina said. When they were alone, she said to Kate, "Are you sure Penny and Ben don't mind babysitting him for the night? And missing your party?"

"Nah, don't worry! I think Penny'll be happy to *not* be at The Den on her night off. Plus, Grayson'll be good practice for when their own bear cub comes," Kate assured her.

Knowing Ben was a bear shifter made Georgina less anxious about leaving Grayson alone for a night. Grayson was prone to uncontrollable shifts around people and kids he didn't know but seemed to be okay around other adult shifters.

"I know you're anxious," Kate said. "But you deserve to enjoy yourself too, you know."

She knew Kate was right, but this would be the first time in months she'd be away from Grayson. If she were truly honest with herself, she was probably more anxious than him. Grayson seemed almost excited by the thought of staying in a cabin in the woods, like it was some camping trip or vacation.

"You look super hot, by the way," Kate said. "I told you that dress would look great."

Georgina laughed nervously. "You're too kind."

"No, really. Curvy girls are in. I wish I had a little more 'cushion for the pushin.'"

She eyed Kate's svelte figure. "You're ridiculous, you know. *You're* perfect."

"I think I need a boob job!" She pushed her breasts together and laughed.

"Are you un 'ployed, Auntie Kate? Like Mommy was when we came here?" Grayson asked as he came up to them, his little backpack in hand.

"What?" Kate asked.

"Because you said you need a job," Grayson said. "Do you need money, Auntie Kate? Is that why you're not wearing a lot of clothes? You can live with us if you need to save money, like when we lived at the castle."

Georgina covered her face in mortification, but Kate laughed out loud. "Oh my precious little man." She picked him up. "I hope someday I can meet a grown man just as sweet as you. But I'm doing fine, Grayson. Thank you for the offer. Now, let's go."

After transferring Grayson's car seat to Kate's car, they drove up to Ben and Penny's cabin in the Blackstone Mountains. It was a detour from town, but Georgina could understand why they would want to live out here. It was beautiful and peaceful, plus their home was gorgeous.

"Wow!" Grayson exclaimed when they exited the car. "It's huge!"

The "cabin" was more like a mansion—it was a two-story log structure with a large stone wraparound porch. The door opened, and Penny walked out and waved to them.

"Penny, thank you so much for offering to watch him," Georgina said as she followed Grayson, who had rushed up to the porch ahead of her.

"It's no trouble at all," the pretty redhead said. "It'll be nice to have him around."

"Where's Ben?" Kate asked.

"Oh, he got called back to work," Penny explained. "But don't worry, he'll be right back."

Georgina tried not to let her apprehension show. Penny was pregnant, after all, and could be feeling emotional, which was why she didn't want to say anything else. She knew what that was like, people thinking she'd be a bad mom. Still, she couldn't help but worry, as Grayson could be a handful. "All right, well, you have my number. Call me for anything." She bent down and gave Grayson a hug and told him to be nice to Penny and not to break anything.

"We'll be all right," Penny said, ruffling Grayson's hair. "I made mac and cheese, plus I have board games and lots of DVDs."

"My favorite!" Grayson exclaimed. "Can we eat now,

please? I'm hungry!"

Georgina laughed. Maybe she was being too paranoid. Grayson would be fine. "All right, I'll be back by eleven. Sybil said she'd bring us home. It is a weekday, after all."

They said their last goodbyes and soon were on their way to The Den, one of the more popular shifter bars in Blackstone. It seemed the party was already in full swing when they got there, since The Den was overflowing with people.

"Late for you own party? Really, Kate?" Sybil admonished when they walked in the door.

"Of course!" Kate said. "I'm always fashionably late. C'mon," she hooked her arm around Georgina's, "the party doesn't *really* start until the birthday girl is here."

Kate brought her around, introducing her to people she didn't know and generally making sure she wasn't alone in some corner like a wallflower. Being around the exuberant Kate could be exhausting and she was glad to find herself at a table with some familiar people, namely, Catherine and Christina Lennox, Sybil, Amelia Walker, and Dutchy Forrester.

"White wine?" Sybil offered.

"No thanks," Georgina said. "I don't drink much." It had been years since she'd had alcohol.

"Shhh, don't let Kate hear you say that," Amelia said.

"She might think it's a challenge," Dutchy warned.

"She'll have you downing tequila in no time," Christina said in a droll voice.

"Did someone say tequila? Because I got a bottle with your names on it." Kate said, popping up from nowhere. "I'm kidding! Christina, stop looking at me like that!" She rolled her eyes. "While I didn't bring any booze, I did bring you Blackstone's bravest!" She pointed to the three men who towered behind her. "They all work at the Blackstone Fire Department. Guys, you already know Christina and Catherine, but that's Sybil, Georgina, Dutchy, and Amelia."

"Hello ladies," the tallest and burliest of the three said. He had dark wavy hair and the bluest eyes Georgina had ever seen. "I'm Will."

"Nice to meet you," the second one said with a wave of his hand. He had dark brown hair and an easy smile. "Eric."

"And I'm Evan," the youngest of them said. He had a boyish, clean-shaven face and light blond hair.

"Sorry, I guess I didn't bring enough guys," Kate said, giving meaningful glances at the four single ladies in the group.

"There's enough of us to go around," Eric said as he winked at Sybil. "I can double up if needed." Sybil rolled her eyes.

Amelia gave a laugh that sounded forced. "I think I see an old high school friend. I should go say hi to her." She slammed back what remained of her wine and walked away. Sybil gave Kate a warning look.

"We're just here to celebrate Kate's birthday," Will said, with a warning glance at Eric. "We don't have any bad intentions, ladies. How about we get you girls your poison of choice?" He nodded to the bar where the row of people was already three deep.

"That would be great," Georgina said. "Just cola for me, please."

The three men took the rest of their orders and walked off to the bar to get their drinks.

"Seriously, Kate?" Sybil said. "*Fire*men?"

"That's perfect for you, right?" Kate said with a snort. "Don't you think they're cute, Dutchy? Georgina?"

"Uh, sure?" Dutchy said.

"And Amelia!" Sybil admonished. "She's not ready. You *know* it."

"She can't mope around in Messina Springs forever because some *loser* broke her heart." Kate placed her elbows on the table and planted her chin on her palms. "I just want her to move back to Blackstone so we can all be together again, like when we were kids." She shrugged and downed Sybil's wine. "Stay away from Eric, but that Evan is a seriously nice guy."

Sybil sighed. "It doesn't matter, anyway. When he finds out who I am and *what* I am, it won't matter. He'll run the other direction, just like every boy I grew up with around here. Maybe what I need to do is move away, like Amelia."

"What you need is a real man," Dutchy said. "One who won't be intimidated by your family name or animal."

"That's hard, considering I'm one of the biggest apex predators in town," Sybil said with an unhappy sigh.

Georgina couldn't help but sympathize with Sybil, about having people intimidated because of who you were related to. Growing up, everyone around her gave her a wide berth. Everyone, that is, except Mark Mills.

"Sorry we took so long, ladies," Will said as they returned. He handed Georgina her soda. "So, Georgina, right? What do you do?"

Georgina took a sip of her drink. Maybe, just for one night. Surely she could enjoy herself and not feel guilty. "I work at Lennox ...."

As the party wore on, Georgina found herself enjoying the

surrounding company. Will Mason was attentive and gorgeous, not to mention, a real gentleman who let her talk about herself and got all her drinks, never letting her glass go empty. He was actually the Fire Chief of the Blackstone F.D., the youngest the department had ever had. He was also divorced and had a son who was a year older than Grayson, so they mostly talked about their kids and being parents.

Yet, Georgina was having a hard time mustering up anything more than a slight interest in Will. Even when he was staring at her with those piercing baby blues, her mind kept circling back to tawny gold eyes. God, she was hopeless. How many times would Luke Lennox have to reject her before her pride took enough of a beating that she would forget about him? And she would probably never get laid again for the rest of her life if she didn't at least *try*.

"So, Georgina," Will said in a low voice as he leaned down closer to her. "I was thinking we should exchange numbers. To set up a playdate or something."

"You mean for Grayson and Mikey, right?" she asked, tilting her head toward him.

He laughed. "Of course. And you know, my sister could babysit them both, too, if you wanted to get dinner."

She sucked in a breath. "I'd like that." She took out her phone from her purse. "I—" She frowned. The screen lit up with a call. It was Penny.

"Oh, sorry, I need to take this." She put the phone to her ear. "Hey Penny, what's up?"

"Oh God, Georgina!" The panic in Penny's voice was evident, even through the crackle of static on her phone. She gave Will an apologetic look and pointed to the phone, then rushed outside of the bar, where it was quiet and the air was cooler and fresher.

"What's wrong, Penny?"

Penny's voice came out in a choked sob. "Georgina ... it's Grayson."

"Penny! Take a deep breath." Her voice was firm but not angry or panicked. "Tell me what happened. Where's Ben?"

"He's been stuck at work, dealing with an emergency. And Grayson and I ... we ... we had dinner and then played board games and watched a couple DVDs. He was fine, I swear. And I laid him down to sleep on the couch and ... he was dreaming and then he shifted! I tried to stop him, but he clawed me and then went out the back."

"He just ... ran away?"

"Oh Georgina, I'm so sorry! I called Ben; he's on the way back."

Fear gripped her like a fist tightening around her chest. Grayson had never just shifted uncontrollably in his sleep, though he'd never been away from her this long, not even before their stay in the lab. She didn't have much of a life, after all, and spent all her free time with Grayson.

"Okay, calm down. Take a deep breath." She didn't want Penny to worry, especially with her delicate condition. "Wait for Ben. I'm on my way."

"I'm so sorry."

"It's not your fault. We'll find him, okay? I'll see you soon." She didn't want to seem rude, but she needed to move quickly and head to the cabin.

She let out a curse as she remembered she didn't drive here. "Oh God," she sobbed. *Grayson, sweetie, please be safe.*

"What's wrong?"

Georgina froze, hearing the rough, familiar voice. She turned around slowly as if unsure if what she had heard was real. When golden eyes stared down at her, she knew he wasn't just a figment of her imagination.

"What's wrong?" Luke repeated.

"I have to go." What was he doing here, anyway? Glancing back at the door to The Den, she realized he was probably on his way to Kate's party. "You should go inside, everyone's in there already."

"Is it your boy?"

"I—" She wanted to tell him to just leave her alone. But those intense eyes seemed to hypnotize her. "He ran away. I dropped him off with Penny, but he shifted while he was asleep."

"You left him alone with Penny to come to a party?"

Anger flared within her at his judgmental tone, but she pushed it away for now. There were more important things. "You're already late for the party. I'm sure Kate wants to see you. I'm going to see if someone can give me a ride—"

"I'll take you," he said, placing a hand at her elbow. His touch sent a tingling up her arm.

"What? You don't—" But he was already dragging her away. "Luke, it's fine. I can ask Sybil or Catherine—"

"I said I'll take you."

Luke led her toward an old white Ford truck parked a couple of feet away. He walked her over to the passenger side and opened the door. She considered protesting and running back to The Den, but she needed to find Grayson and each second she wasted meant he could be closer to danger.

"Thank you," she said curtly as he hopped into the driver's side. The slamming of the door and the engine roaring to life was the only answer she got.

Georgina massaged her temple as she looked out the window. This was going to be a long night.

CHAPTER FOUR

LUKE SHIFTED the gear higher as he sped up. Though Georgina's face was turned away from him and she remained silent, he could see the tension in her body as her hands wrung together on her lap. He also couldn't ignore the expanse of silky skin the dress showed off, from her legs up to her mid-thigh, and the bare shoulders and arms. He tore his gaze away from her luscious body and kept it on the road.

Mine, the lion inside him growled.

The animal was furious at Luke. First, for rejecting her and then staying away from her. It had been difficult to say no to her when she offered to cook him dinner. Since then, he vowed to stay away, and he did. At least during the day. At night, he continued to watch over her, even following her when she moved out of the castle. Her house was now a regular detour from his usual patrolling routes.

He wasn't going to show up for Kate's party. It wasn't like she was expecting him even though she had texted him the invite. But when he saw Georgina walk out of the house with Kate as he watched her house, he knew where she'd be.

And so now, his lion was fuming at him, for letting that man flirt with her at the party. Oh, he'd been there the whole night, sulking in the corner, watching her, seething as Fire Chief Will Mason cozied up to her, while she laughed at his jokes and listened to his stories. He wanted to rip the other man's hands off as he gave her small touches on the arm and shoulders. And tear his head off for leaning down and whispering in her ear. Mason was a bear shifter, but Luke was pretty sure he could take him.

But he didn't do anything. Because Georgina wasn't his.

When she ran out of The Den he knew something was wrong and had to follow her out. Her cub was lost, and like a good mom, she of course needed to do the right thing. Still, his lion was mad at him for not comforting her while she was obviously in distress.

I'm already helping her, aren't I?

The lion roared, and he glanced over at Georgina again. The growing tension was so thick he could cut it with a knife.

What the hell d'you want me to do? I don't know shit about women.

His entire life, there had only been two women he had ever truly cared about: Riva and Sybil. For some reason, a long-forgotten memory popped into his brain. He was maybe nine or ten and he'd been called to the Principal's office for pushing Jenny Abernathy in the playground. Riva came to the school and after a long chat with the principal, she brought him home for the day.

Luke had prepared himself for a scolding, but Riva took him aside and spoke gently to him. "Luke, you know, if you like someone, you don't have to hurt them to get their attention."

He remembered growing embarrassed. How did Riva know?

"If you meet a girl who feels special to you," she continued. "You can tell her. But if you're too shy, you can show her by doing nice things for her."

Luke couldn't quite recall what had happened with Jenny afterwards. Or why he suddenly remembered that incident from *before*. Before he had irrevocably broken Riva's heart.

He buried the memory and those thoughts as they had arrived at the cabin. Ben's Jeep pulled into the driveway just ahead of them. Luke hadn't even turned the engine off before Georgina dashed out of his truck. He followed her, plodding up the steps to the front door. Ben was already there, comforting his wife as she sobbed and held a towel to her arm.

Georgina let out a gasp. When Penny saw her, her eyes widened. "I'm so sorry! I let him—"

"It's not your fault," Georgina said, cutting her off. "Are you hurt? Did he scratch you?"

"It's not bad." Penny shrank away as Georgina tried to look at her arm. "Grayson's been gone for an hour. We need to start looking for him."

"Which way did he go?" Luke asked.

Ben's gaze went from Luke to Georgina and then back to him. He looked like he wanted to say something, but remained quiet as his wife began to explain what had happened.

"... and then he went out the back door. I must have left it open. I'm so stupid!"

"Shh, sweetheart, no one blames you," Ben said.

"I'll take the rear and the east side," Luke said, then turned to Ben. "You take the front and the west. But call the Rangers first before you go, tell them to keep an eye out for the cub."

"Good idea," Ben said with a nod. He kissed Penny on the forehead. "You girls stay here."

"I want to help look!" Georgina protested.

"You need to stay here," Luke said. "If he comes back first or one of us brings him home, he'll need you."

She looked like she wanted to protest, but after a second, she nodded her head.

"We'll find him," Luke said. "He can't have gone that far." With a nod at Ben, he turned and walked to the back of the cabin, slipping his shirt and jeans off. He called his lion to the surface, letting it take over his body as a series of pops and growls signaled his change. Once he was in full lion form, he sniffed around the back door, picking up the boy's scent. He wished Nathan were here, as his wolf was excellent at tracking down scents. But his lion was good enough for now, plus he had other abilities.

The scent led him toward the woods beyond the backyard. He followed it and though it was getting fainter as it mixed in with other scents, he used his enhanced vision to scan the area for anything unusual.

There. A broken branch. Some trampled grass. If the cub was startled or scared, it would leave an easy trail to follow.

The lion padded deeper into the woods, scanning for more signs. Then, he heard it. A soft cry, almost like a bark. The sound sent the lion's hackles rising, and it followed the sound until it reached the source.

Luke knew this area. There was a drop-off that was difficult to see, even if one was being careful. He peered over the side and sure enough, there was a bear cub desperately trying to claw its way up to the edge.

He quickly transformed back into his human skin. "It's all right," he said in the gentlest voice he could muster. "I'll get you out." As he got on his stomach and reached down, the cub swiped at him and razor-sharp claws dug into this arm, leaving a streak of red.

"I'm here to help," he said, ignoring the pain. "C'mon, now." He pushed down farther until his hands grabbed under the cub's arms and lifted him up.

To his surprise, it didn't fight him. It was probably just scared. The cub wrapped its furry arms around his neck and pushed its snout into his shoulder.

He breathed a sigh and ran a hand down the cub's back. "You okay, buddy? Can you change back?" The cub mewled unhappily. "It's fine. Take your time. I'll bring you back to your momma now."

As Luke walked toward the cabin, Grayson was slowly changing back to human form. He shifted the child's weight to one arm as he hopped into his discarded jeans on the porch, and by the time he finished buttoning them up, Grayson was fully human.

He heard the front door fly open and as he turned the corner, Georgina was already running toward them.

"Grayson!" she cried, reaching out to him. As soon as the boy saw his mother, he wiggled out of Luke's grasp and dove into his mother's arms.

"I'm sorry, Mommy," he said, sniffling back his tears. "I had a bad dream. The bad man was back, and he was coming to take me into the cage again."

She kissed his temple. "It's okay, shh ... you're here now." She peered up at Luke, a grateful look on her face. "Thank you," she said. "You saved him. Again."

He shrugged. "It was easy to find him. But you really

shouldn't leave him alone, not without someone fit enough to watch out for him." Juvenile shifters had a hard time controlling their animals. It was perfectly normal, but Penny by herself wouldn't have known what to do. Where had Ben been?

Georgina's mouth opened, but nothing came out. Her nostrils flared and her lips pursed together. "Excuse me," she mumbled as she turned away and went inside the cabin. It was difficult to ignore the flash of hurt in her eyes before she went frosty.

"Georgina," he called. "Do—" The door slammed shut before he could say anything else. He stood there for a few seconds, frowning at the door. It opened again, and he jumped back at the force.

Georgina, sans Grayson, marched out. This time, her face was red, though there was a steely determination on her face. "You found my son and for that I'm grateful," she began. "But you don't get to judge me. Not when you don't know me or my son."

Huh? "Excuse me?"

Her eyes blazed. "I know what you're thinking. That I'm a terrible mother for leaving my son with a near stranger, who was pregnant and alone. I thought Ben would be here, but he was called away. I was going to forget the whole party and stay with Grayson, but I didn't want to hurt Penny's feelings, not when she's hormonal and nervous and sensitive about the whole motherhood thing. Believe me, I know how it feels when people think you're not capable enough, just because you're a woman on your own."

Oh shit. "Georgina—"

"And another thing!" She poked her finger at his chest. It didn't hurt, but at the same time, it *did*. "What I do in my personal time is none of your business! If I want to go out and have fun with my friends, I make sure I take care of my son first. I don't need to ask permission from anyone or worry about what judgmental assholes think."

Her voice, shaky as it was, cut into him. Clearly, she misunderstood what he had said, just now and earlier tonight when he asked if she had left her son just to go to Kate's party. She deserved to have fun, of course. He just couldn't stop the jealousy from rearing its ugly green head, not after seeing her with Will.

He didn't know how long they stood there, staring at each other, but it must have been long enough because she let out a huff, pivoted on her heel, and marched back into the cabin before slamming the door—again—in his face.

Fuck. He messed up. Big fucking time.

"You okay?" Ben asked as he walked around the corner from the other side of the wraparound porch.

"Yeah," he said automatically. However, his lion was roaring at him in fury, for angering their mate.

Ben sensed it too and approached him carefully. "She's pretty pissed at you."

"I tend to have that effect on people."

Ben scratched the back of his head. "I should go in and check on them. I'll probably end up driving them home. Anything you want to talk about?"

"No," he said. "Nothing to talk about." He turned away from Ben and strode over to his truck without saying another word.

CHAPTER FIVE

"GRAYSON!" Georgina called as she stood in the living room, purse slung over her shoulder and keys in her hand. "Let's go young man!"

A muffled shout answered her back, and she rolled her eyes. Another normal weekday morning. She supposed she should be grateful, considering what happened last night. Grayson had been more scared of coming back to the cabin, after realizing what he'd done. He had been afraid of getting punished for hurting Penny, but Ben had explained it was all right. Penny was fine, aside from her scratch, which was now healing. After that, Grayson had seemed mollified, and he apologized to Penny, who, bless her heart, accepted it and even gave him a big hug to show she wasn't afraid of him.

Georgina was glad Grayson was okay; he even slept until morning without incident. It was her, on the other hand, who had tossed and turned the whole night.

What had possessed her to go off the rails on Luke like that? Staying up until the sun rose hadn't helped her find an inkling of a clue. Luke had saved Grayson—twice now—and yet she screamed at him like some lunatic. She cringed at the memory. She had been relieved when she saw him bringing back Grayson, but then he called her out on leaving him alone and she lost it. She'd had enough of the judgy stares from people for most of Grayson's life; she didn't need it from him, too.

Anyway, what did it matter? She would never see Luke Lennox again, not if she could help it.

"Grayson!" she called again. "I'm going to be out in the car. If you're not out in thirty seconds, I'm leaving without you!"

As she yanked the door open, her heart nearly jumped out of her chest at what she saw. Or rather *who*. Luke Lennox was standing on the small stoop of her porch, looking like he belonged there.

"Wh-what are you doing here?" She grabbed onto the doorjamb to steady herself as her knees nearly buckled. In the early morning daylight, he looked even more handsome. His long hair was tied back, and his beard looked neatly-trimmed. The green v-neck shirt he wore wasn't tight-fitting, but still showed off his tattooed arms and wide chest, which narrowed all the way down to his waist. She forced herself to look up at his face before her eyes moved any lower.

"I'm sorry. For what I said. But you misunderstood my words."

Misunderstood his words? Oh, they sounded perfectly clear to her. She crossed her arms over her chest. "Is this one of those 'I'm sorry, but' apologies?"

He let out a grunt and took a step closer to her porch, then shoved his hands into his pockets. "Look, what I said yesterday wasn't meant to judge you. I'm just not good with words."

She stared at him, stunned.

He took another step forward. "What happened to Grayson was perfectly normal. You just didn't know how to deal with it."

Georgina was intrigued. She thought she was going to get a lecture that she had somehow damaged her son. "What do you mean?"

"All shifters go through that phase. He's around the right age when your animal starts to wrestle with you for control and wants to test your boundaries. Nocturnal shiftings aren't unusual, but neither you nor Penny were equipped to handle it. How could you? Neither of you ever went through it."

"I thought Ben would be there," she said, her shoulders sagging.

"He should have been, but he didn't know it would be a problem."

How did he get so close? Luke was inches from her now and her gut tightened being this near to him. It was a strange reaction. "So, what do I do?"

"He needs someone to help him through it, explain it all. Ideally, that would be his mom or dad."

"Oh." She felt deflated. Of course she couldn't do that for him. And Mark was long gone. What was she supposed to do now?

"I could help him."

Her head snapped up so fast, she felt dizzy. "Y-you? But you're a lion and he's a bear."

"And a dragon taught me," he said. "If you'd feel more comfortable having Ben do it—"

"No!" The protest came a bit too strong and she cursed silently. "I mean, I don't want to bother him. Between his job and Penny, he's got enough to worry about."

"We should start soon. I'll be here at three tomorrow."

"Tomorrow?"

"Yeah. I'll see you then." He turned around.

Georgina swallowed a gulp. "Uh. I guess? Wait—" She barely blinked and he was gone. Damn shifter speed.

"Mommy. Mommy!"

She jumped when she felt a small hand tug at her skirt. "Oh, Grayson. Sorry, sweetie, I didn't see you."

He frowned and took a deep breath. "Was Luke here?"

"How did you—" Of course. Shifter smell. "Yeah."

His eyes widened. "Why didn't he stay? I haven't said sorry yet."

"Sorry?"

He nodded. "I scratched him, too. While he rescued me from the cliff."

"He rescued …." Oh God, she didn't even know. "You can say sorry tomorrow."

"Tomorrow?"

She nodded. "Let's get into the car. I'll tell you all about it."

Georgina adjusted the throw pillows on her couch for what seemed like the 127th time. With her hands on her hips, she examined them again. *Nope*. They definitely looked better on the sides.

God, this is crazy. She sank down on the couch and slapped her hands on her knees. She'd vacuumed at least two times, wiped down the kitchen counter three times, not to mention, changed her outfit four times. Which was a feat in and of itself as she really only owned a few pieces of clothing. She smoothed her hands down her jean shorts and then brushed an imaginary piece of lint off her white t-shirt. She had settled on this outfit because it was simple and didn't seem like she was trying too hard. She did put on some makeup and fixed up her hair, so it fell in waves down her shoulders. But it wasn't like she was trying to look pretty for Luke.

She grabbed a pillow and buried her face in it. "Ugh!" Why was she so anxious? Just because Luke was coming over? He probably wouldn't even care what she wore or what state the house was in. *He's here for Grayson*, she reminded herself. *Not me.*

The sound of the doorbell made her jump and toss the pillow to the floor. *Oh for heaven's sake! Calm the fudge down!* With a deep breath, she walked to the front door.

"Hi, Luke," she greeted as she opened the door.

"Hello," he said with a nod.

Oh dear. Her heart went thump-thump-thump at the sight of Luke in his tight black shirt, khaki cargo pants, and boots. His hair was loose today, falling down to his shoulders. She averted her eyes from his well-muscled chest and shoulders before he realized she was ogling him.

"So, can I come in?" he asked, raising a blond brow.

"Oh right. Please." As she turned away from him, she visibly winced in embarrassment. "Why don't you have a seat? I'll call—"

"He's here! He's here! I heard him!" Grayson's shouts rang down from the hall that led to his bedroom. He zoomed into the living room, stopping inches from Luke. His mouth was open as he looked up at the lion shifter, craning his neck. "Are you really here to teach me shifter stuff?"

Luke bent down to his level, planting his elbows on his knees. "Only if you want me to."

His face turned remorseful. "Will you help me, so I won't hurt people? Like I did with Miss Penny? And you?"

He held out his arm to the boy. "It was just a scratch. All healed up, see?"

Grayson traced his small hand across Luke's forearm. "I want to learn."

Luke nodded. "Good. We'll start now." He stood up to his full height and turned to Georgina. "Your backyard should be plenty of space, if that's okay."

"Of course." *How did he know they had a backyard?* It wasn't visible from the street and there was only forest behind her house. "You guys can go ahead, and I'll watch from the porch. Can I get you some water? Soda?"

"I'm fine. But." He hesitated. "Just so you know, I may have to shift as well."

"Okay."

"And since I don't like to rip my clothes, I'll be taking them off first."

"Sure. That's great." *Oh crap.* Heat flooded her cheeks. "You know what? I suddenly remembered I have to do some … vacuuming." She turned around and walked to the broom closet to take out the vacuum cleaner. "You boys have fun. Or whatever. I'll be here. Inside. Waiting." Oh, she would be cringing at the memory of this for weeks. No, *years.* She imagined being at Grayson's wedding someday and right in the middle of her speech, she'd recall how she basically told Luke Lennox she was going to watch him as he displayed his naughty bits.

"Uh, Georgina? Are you okay?"

How long had she been standing there? "I'm fine," she said in a cheery voice. "You boys go on with your lesson. I'll have dinner ready when you're done."

As soon as she heard the door to the backyard close, Georgina cringed, her fingernails digging into her palms as she curled them into fists. *Get a grip*, she told herself. Luke was here to teach her son important life lessons, not get ogled by an undersexed single mom. From now on, she'd have to keep all thoughts of Luke to PG. She glanced out the window and saw him take his shirt off. Okay, maybe PG-13.

As Georgina busied herself with vacuuming for the third time, she heard roars and growls occasionally, but she told herself that was normal. Even though she hardly knew him, she knew she could trust Luke. After putting away the vacuum, she headed to the kitchen to start dinner.

She wasn't a gourmet chef or anything, but Georgina thought she was an okay cook. She put together mac and cheese for Grayson and fried chicken and mashed potatoes for the adults. Peeking out the window, she saw a glimpse of Luke's naked muscled back and the upper curve of his firm ass as he slipped his jeans on. Oh dear Lord, she was dangerously close to R-rated territory.

When she heard the sliding glass door open, she headed to the living room. "How was it, sweetie?" she asked as Luke and Grayson walked inside.

"Mommy! Mommy!" Grayson said excitedly, running up to hug her legs. "It was awesome. Luke was teaching me how to control my bear. I wasn't very good at first, but we practiced a few times."

"That's sounds great," she said, not really sure what that meant. "Are you going to show your bear who's boss now?"

"That's not how it works, Mommy!" Grayson said, then looked up at Luke. "Luke says I'm in charge, but I gotta work with my bear. It knows things too, and sometimes, you gotta listen to it. I'm still having a hard time, but Luke says I'll get better with practice. Right, Luke?"

Luke nodded at Grayson. "Just keep practicing. You're a

smart and strong boy. You'll make your mom proud someday."

Georgina's heart just about melted. "Well, dinner's ready." She cleared her throat. "Why don't you guys wash up and we can sit down?"

Luke frowned. "I should go."

"You can't go!" Grayson grabbed his hand and tugged at it. "Please stay for dinner. Please, Luke? Mommy makes the best mac and cheese!"

"It comes out of the blue box," she confessed. "But I made chicken and mashed potatoes."

Luke seemed to hesitate for a moment. "All right. Show me where I can wash up."

"Yay!" Grayson raised his fist in triumph. "Come with me! I'll show you the bathroom. You can use my strawberry soap if you want!"

Georgina watched as Luke lumbered away, dragged by a very enthusiastic Grayson, who continued to chatter as they disappeared into the hallway.

As soon as she finished getting the food on the table, Luke and Grayson came back, and they sat around the dinner table and began to eat.

"Grayson, sweetie, slow down," Georgina said, feeling embarrassed as her son shoveled spoon after spoon of mac and cheese into his mouth. "I don't want you to choke."

"He burned a lot of calories," Luke said. "Changing back and forth does that." She noticed Luke himself had a big pile of food on his plate. Good thing she had made a lot of extras.

"Good to know," she laughed. "Looks like he'll be eating me out of house and home for the next few years."

"Just be prepared," Luke said. "And at least you only have one boy."

"Oh, that's right," Georgina said as she swallowed a bite of chicken. "Your parents had to raise three boys."

"They're not my parents," Luke said in a flat tone.

"Oh. I just thought … Catherine said you were adopted." The tension in the air grew thick, and Georgina realized it must have been a sensitive subject.

Grayson let out a loud burp. Georgina had never been so thankful for her son's behavior, as it dispersed the tension. "Yummy! Can I have some more, Mommy?"

"You can have as much as you want," she said, quickly piling his plate with more mac and cheese.

Luke cleared his throat. "Grayson, you should eat more than just noodles. It'll help you grow stronger."

"Then I want some chicken and 'tatoes, too, Mommy." He gave Luke a big grin. "I want to grow up big and strong, just like Luke."

Dinner continued, and Georgina was happy to let Grayson keep chatting away, just so she didn't have to talk. Finally, they finished their meal and despite his protests, Georgina could see Grayson's eyes getting droopy.

"I think someone needs an early bedtime."

"But Mommy! I wanted to play with Luke some more."

"I think we're done for the day," Luke declared. "I told you, you're doing great. You can practice on your own now."

"But," he let out a big yawn, "I want you to teach me more."

Georgina chuckled and got up from her chair. "You've done a lot today, sweetie. You need rest to grow big and strong. Right, Luke?"

"Yup."

Grayson sulked but allowed Georgina to pick him up. "All right." Another yawn escaped. "Will you tuck me in, Mommy?"

She kissed his forehead. "Of course. Say good night and thank you to Luke.

"Good night, Luke," Grayson said. "And thank you."

"You're welcome," Luke replied with a nod.

She gave Luke a tight smile before she left the living room and walked to Grayson's room. He was fast asleep by the time she got him dressed and tucked in his bed. When she walked back out to the living room, it was empty, though the dining table had been cleared. There was no sign of Luke, but she heard sounds coming from the kitchen.

Much to her surprise, she found him there, cleaning the plates and loading up the dishwasher. *Single, handsome, and knows how to clean up, too.* Why no woman had snapped him up by now was a mystery to her. Maybe he wasn't into women? As she stared at his well-formed backside when he bent down to put glasses in the dishwasher, she stifled a groan and congratulated all the men on the planet if that was true.

"You don't have to clean up," she finally said.

He stood up to his full height, closed the dishwasher door, and turned back to her. "You already made dinner. It was delicious, by the way, in case I didn't tell you."

"Thank you, though I don't have any formal training or anything. I just taught myself a few recipes."

He wiped his hands on a towel and grabbed some clean glasses from the counter. "Even better. You worked for it."

She was tongue-tied at his words, and her breath caught in her throat when he stalked toward her. God, she couldn't get used to how big he was. And he was coming even closer. She staggered back, her butt hitting the counter behind her. Luke raised his arms, trapping her in between them. From here, she could smell him—all sweaty and manly and it was driving her wild. "Luke."

"Georgina," he whispered. "I need—"

Her eyes flew open. "Yes?"

"—to put these glasses away."

"Huh?"

He lifted the glasses in front of her face. "They go in the cabinet behind you, right?"

"Uh, sure." She stepped aside. It was like a bucket of ice water had been dumped on her head, though her cheeks burned like the heat of a thousand suns. *Georgina, you idiot.* If Luke didn't bat for the same team, then it was obvious: he just wasn't into her.

"So," he began as he closed the cabinet doors. "I think Grayson should be okay. He just needed someone to tell him what to do when his bear gets testy." He turned around, leaned his hip on the counter, and crossed his arms over his chest, the muscles flexing under the inked skin. "Let him practice when you're alone. The more he's comfortable in his bear form, the better it will be for him in the long run." He handed her a piece of paper. "Here's my number. Call me if he loses control again."

She took it. "Thank you. For teaching him and the advice."

"It's nothing."

"So, uhh, would you like to stay for some coffee?"

"It's getting late. And I have stuff to do." Luke uncrossed his arms. "Thank you for dinner. I'll see myself out. Lock your door."

Georgina stared after him, watching him walk away from her. She heard the door open and then close again. She let out a breath. Whatever *this* was—her fascination with Luke Lennox—it had to stop now.

She didn't want to say it out loud, but there was something about the sight of Luke and Grayson together that made her heart wrench. *No, I can't think like that.* Luke had done them a favor. He helped Grayson to prevent other people from getting hurt. That was it. She couldn't venture into more dangerous thoughts because Grayson's heart would get broken if he grew too attached to Luke or to Blackstone.

CHAPTER SIX

LUKE COULDN'T GET out of Georgina's house fast enough. He yanked open the door of his truck and got in. He slipped the key into the ignition, turned it on before he could even settle in, then backed out of the driveway.

He gripped the wheel tight as he turned onto the highway. What was he thinking, coming to her house, and offering to teach her son like that? He knew it was a bad idea, yet he had been anticipating it all day. He had even arrived thirty minutes early, but parked his car two blocks away, sitting in the driver's seat, contemplating canceling the whole thing. But he knew the boy needed someone to teach him how to get a hold of his bear, or he'd risk the lives of those around him. Feral shifters were no joke; he should know, as he had nearly gone crazy himself.

Coming here today had dredged up the old memories of Hank teaching him the same thing he had taught the boy today. The happy times. Before *that* day. The one he'd been trying to forget most of his life.

He shouldn't have come, but he couldn't let the boy

continue hurting anyone, not when he could help. And Georgina?

Mine.

He gave his lion a scornful laugh. She didn't deserve him, the baggage he carried, or the pain that would surely come from being his mate. He wasn't sure he even had a heart to give her.

After the long, silent drive, Luke finally reached his cabin, deep in the Blackstone Mountains. The one-room cabin had been run down and half the roof was caved in when he bought it with every cent he saved from working in the mines. Over the years, he'd done all the repairs himself, and though it wasn't much, it was all his, bought and paid for by his own sweat.

He parked his truck and went inside. It was time. Time for him to go out and roam the woods. The stakes were higher now and there was real danger about. He couldn't forget that.

But, God, he didn't think he'd be this tired. He'd never felt *this* tired, like there was a heavy stone pressing down on him. Shifting back and forth expended a lot of energy. Between teaching Grayson, brawling with his own lion, and fighting his attraction to Georgina, he was spent. He sat down on his bed and kicked his shoes off. Maybe a quick nap would help. He closed his eyes. *Just a couple of minutes.*

The dream settled over him like a warm blanket. But it wasn't just a dream.

It was a stupid fight, really. Some bully teasing another kid. Brian Campbell. Grizzly shifter. He was stuffing some poor kid into a locker when Luke saw him and decided enough was enough. He grabbed Brian by the neck and pulled him away, slamming him against the wall so hard he made a dent in the concrete. A crowd had gathered to watch the fight.

Brian was big, even for his age, but Luke was smarter and stronger. Kicking his ass had been the best feeling in the world.

"Fuck you, Luke!" Brian said as he spat blood onto the floor. "Who do you think you are? The protector of Blackstone or something? You think you're better than all of us? Just because of your parents? You're not even a *real* Lennox!"

That made him see red. He shifted into his lion and pounced on Brian, ready to bite his head off. In that moment, he had broken one of the more sacred unspoken rules in the shifter world: you never use your animal to hurt someone when they were down or in human form. The last grips of his control were barely there, and he held on until the school marshals came and took them away to the special detention center in the school, one built for out-of-control shifter students.

Both Hank and Riva came to the school, which told him exactly how serious the situation was. They said nothing when they picked him up and drove him back to Blackstone Castle.

"What were you thinking?" Hank was in a rage and the temperature in the room dropped at least ten degrees. This was the first time he'd ever seen his father angry. Firm, yes, but never angry.

"They want to expel you, Luke," Riva said, her voice shaky. "For hurting that boy."

He seethed, but said nothing. His eyes remained fixed ahead. This wasn't fair. Brian was the one who was hurting that kid. All Luke wanted to do was help.

"You shifted and then tried to bite him? While he was down?" Hank's face was red. "You know we don't do that. That's not our way. Didn't I teach you better?"

"Luke, tell us what happened," Riva soothed. She placed a hand on his shoulder, making him flinch. "It's all right. I know you wouldn't do that if you didn't have a reason."

Hank sank down on the couch and placed his face in his hands. "I can't believe you're going to be expelled. From the Lucas Lennox Memorial High School. You know we named you after him, right?"

Luke gritted his teeth. "But I'm not a Lennox."

Hank whipped his head toward him. "Excuse me?"

Luke stood up, fists at his sides. "I'm. *Not*. A. Lennox!"

"Luke!" Riva admonished. "Don't say that!"

"But it's true," he raged. "I'm not. Everyone knows I'm not. Why do you keep pretending I am?"

"Sit down, young man," Hank said, his eyes glowing.

"Why did you bring me here anyway? Why did you even bother adopting me?" He stood his ground. "You should have sent me back to my pride!"

Riva let out a gasp and then looked at Hank. His face remained passive.

"What happened to me?"

"Luke, we found you—"

"I know that!" He gritted his teeth. "But afterwards? Did you really try to find them? And there was no trace anywhere? And no one would take me in?"

"Luke, please—"

He saw the look pass between Hank and Riva again. They were hiding something. "What really happened? To me? To them?"

Riva hesitated. "Luke, we wanted to tell you—"

"Don't," Hank said, cutting Riva off. "He's not ready."

"Wait, so you knew what happened to them? To my pride?

My family?" Riva and Hank didn't say a word, but they didn't need to. Their silence said it all. "Tell me."

"No!" Hank said. "Not now."

Luke felt his lion coming to the surface, and his hands turned to claws. "You tell me now or—" He lunged at Hank, but the dragon shifter was too fast. He easily evaded Luke, who went crashing into the wall.

"Get up," Hank said, towering over him.

Luke spat, but slowly got up to his feet. Years of pent up rage seemed to flow out of him. Growing up, he knew he was different from Matthew, Jason, and Sybil. It would have been easy to ignore if they were human, but so starkly obvious as shifters. "If you didn't want to send me back to them, you should have left me to die."

"Lucas Lennox!" Hank shouted, and the temperature dropped below freezing. "You don't mean that. Look at what you've done to your mother."

Riva was curled up on the couch, her body shaking as great sobs escaped her throat and tears flowed down her pale cheeks.

"Apologize to her," Hank commanded. "Now."

His lion roared, rebelling against the dragon as it tried to wrestle for dominance. "You can't tell me what to do. You're not my father," he said in a flat voice. "And she's not my mother." He turned away, ignoring Riva's cries and Hank's angry shouts. He disappeared into the night, letting his lion take over their skin, tucking himself and the hurt he felt deep inside him.

He left, determined to find out the truth for himself, but never ended up finding it. It was hopeless. He followed every clue he could. Spent weeks on the road, doing odd jobs or hunting to feed himself, sleeping in the woods or the city streets. But it was hopeless. The trail went cold somewhere in the Pacific Northwest. With no other leads, he had no choice but to go back to the only home he ever knew.

Luke's eyes flew open, and when he looked outside the window, he saw the faint light of daybreak filtering through. "Damn," he cursed as he ran his hand down his face. Morning already. He missed the night's patrol.

He got up from his bed and stretched. "Fucking memories." He wanted them buried deep, so he could pretend it never happened. But it seemed they were determined to surface.

"Goddamn."

There was something else. It had seemed insignificant back then, but now, it seemed clear as day. There was a nagging feeling inside him, telling him to find out more. And he knew exactly how he was going to do it.

The drive to South Blackstone would be a long one, which is why he left as soon as he could. He also stopped by Rosie's to pick up some freshly baked pastries and coffee. He didn't know what to expect, but he suspected an offering was in order.

After being gone for over a year, Riva reached out to him as soon as he came back. Luke knew she would, as he had come back and asked James Walker for a job at the mines. She came to work, but he turned her away and refused every invitation to come back to the castle. They all wanted him back, to pretend nothing had happened, and that they were one big happy family again.

Well, *almost* everyone, anyway.

Jason, who had been closest to Riva, was the only one who never sought him out. He was the one who gave him the cold shoulder at the events he did show up at. Luke suspected Jason knew more than his other siblings about how much he had hurt Riva.

And now, as he stood outside Jason's loft, he only hoped that the dragon's animosity had lessened over the years. In fact, ever since Luke had helped him get together with his mate, that simmering loathing Jason had around him seemed to dissipate. These days, he was almost cheery.

"What do you want?" Jason asked, bleary eyed and impatient when he answered the door. He wasn't cheery this morning, but it *was* seven a.m. on a Sunday.

"Do I smell pastries? And coffee?" Christina's head popped up from behind Jason. "Luke?"

He held up the two big bags. "These are fresh. From Rosie's."

"Oooh!" She made grabby hands at him and took the bags. "Well, come on in then."

Jason shot him a suspicious look but moved aside to let him in. "The lion comes bearing gifts," he said as Christina began to arrange the pastries and coffee on the dining table. "To what do we owe the pleasure?"

Luke huffed. "I won't take up too much of your time, so I'll come out and say it. I need your help."

"Of course. What do you need?" Christina asked.

"I want you to find information on my pride."

Christina raised a brow. "Your pride?"

"Yes."

Jason took a step forward, his eyes narrowing. "Is this about what happened? When we were teens? Because I swear to God, if Mom gets—"

"This has nothing to do with Riva," he said. After all these years, why did he want to know about his past? "When I went looking for them, I didn't find anything. But I didn't have the resources we have now. And maybe it's all connected." It was a hunch, something that had been building inside him. And until the memories resurfaced last night, he didn't see the connection.

"Wait, what are you saying, Luke?" Christina's brows knitted together. "Did you remember something? Do you think The Organization had something to do with what happened when you were young?"

Luke glanced over at Jason, who shrugged. Of course he would tell Christina. "I think so. I went to look for them. I was gone for almost a year. Followed the trail back to Washington. I came to this town, it was called South Bend. I spent a couple days busing tables at a diner when I heard these old timers talking about an unsolved case from a few years ago. There was a family of shifters there. Armstrongs. They lived in a compound and one day, they all just disappeared."

"Were they lion shifters? Your family?" Christina asked.

"Tried talking to 'em, but it had been so long, they couldn't remember. They said they might have been lions or some type of big cat." He shrugged. "I never got to confirm. I went to the police. They didn't have any records of the family, and no one filed a police report nor was their disappearance investigated." The trail went cold from there and that's when he had decided to come back to Blackstone.

"Not unusual," Jason said with a frown. "No one cares much for our kind."

"Yeah, but there was no trace of them," Luke said. "Nothing. Not even a mention in the newspaper or filings with the local property tax office. It's like they were erased from the earth. And when you mentioned the fact that the Verona Mills cops were crooked—"

"The Organization definitely could have bribed the local police in South Bend," Christina finished. "It's possible." She tapped a finger on her chin. "All right. I'll see what I can do. I'll let our analysts in Lykos know to start searching for any mentions of a family of shifters in Washington."

"Thank you," he said. "Enjoy the pastries. I'll see myself out." He turned on his heel and walked out the door. As he walked into the hallway, he felt a hand on his shoulder.

"You know, if there's anything you need to talk about, I'm here." Jason's hand was heavy, but for some reason, it made him feel lighter. "We're all here."

"I know." He gently removed Jason's hand. "I'll see you around."

The elevator doors opened, and he stepped inside.

Jason didn't turn away, but remained outside, the doors closing as he waved. "See you."

CHAPTER SEVEN

"READY TO GO, SWEETIE?" Georgina asked Grayson.

Grayson looked up at his mother. "All right, Mommy." He got up from the floor and began picking up his things. Georgina turned back to her computer and turned off the monitor. *Finally*. It was almost seven p.m. and she was ready to go home.

"Sorry for keeping you," Matthew said as he stepped out of his office. He glanced over at Grayson. "How's he doing? Is he liking the daycare?"

Georgina nodded. "Oh yeah. I almost couldn't get him to come back up here when they closed. I think he's in love with Irene," she said with a chuckle, referring to the young woman who ran the daycare. "And he enjoys being with the other shifter kids." Having never been around shifters his age, Grayson was excited that he was finally around other children like him. In fact, she'd never seen Grayson look forward to going to any kind of daycare. He'd made so many friends already, and it had only been a few days since he started going.

"That's great," Matthew said. "I'm glad he can finally go. Taking a hold of your shifter side can be challenging, but it's normal to struggle at that age."

"That's what Luke said."

Matthew immediately turned to her and gave her a strange look. "Luke? As in, *my brother* Luke?"

Heat spread over her cheeks. "Uh, yeah. He came over last Saturday and taught Grayson how to control his bear. He said your father taught him."

Matthew seemed stunned. "Yeah, he did. So, Luke came to your house?"

"Uh-huh." Oh dear. She didn't know if that was supposed to be a secret. Was there some kind of rule in Lennox about fraternization with the bosses' family? "I'm sure he was doing it to make sure Grayson didn't hurt anyone." She quickly explained to Matthew what had happened with Penny. "I hope that was okay. I never thought to ask you if there were any regulations—"

"You're not in trouble," Matthew said. "I just …." He shook his head. "Never mind. It's nothing. And don't worry. If Luke wants … to hang out, you guys are free to do so."

Her cheeks got even hotter. "Oh no! It's not like that. I mean, he's not interested or anything."

"Oh yeah?" Matthew raised a dark brow. "How about you?"

"Mommy, I'm ready!" Grayson announced as he popped up beside her.

"Oh, thank God! Er," she gave a laugh, "I mean, good. I'm starving. Maybe we can swing by the diner for dinner?"

"Yeah!" Grayson raised his fist. "Can I have a cheeseburger and fries and a milkshake?"

"Whatever you want." He did save her from the fifth

degree from her boss, after all. "Shall we?"

They all walked out of the building together to the nearly empty parking lot. Matthew escorted them to their car, which was a few rows away, and they said their goodnights before he went to his car. She strapped Grayson into his car seat and drove to the diner. As soon as they arrived, the friendly-looking waitress led them to a booth and handed them their menus.

It was nice to be able to treat Grayson to a meal like this. Back in Wyoming, her salary had barely been enough to get them through the month. Even a trip to the local burger joint was for special occasions only.

But now, she could afford to indulge him like this more frequently. She told Grayson to order whatever he wanted, and so he did—a cheeseburger, fries, and a strawberry milk-shake. She ordered the same, and they shared a banana split for dessert, though he mostly finished it.

Needless to say, Grayson was already groggy by the time she paid the bill and carried him back to the car and put him in his seat. He was fast asleep by the time she pulled out of the diner parking lot.

As she pulled out onto the highway, a truck came up close to her tail. It didn't seem out of the ordinary at the freeway entrance since she slowed down, but the vehicle was so close to her now, its headlights were blinding her in the rearview mirror.

Tilting the mirror, she saw Grayson still fast asleep. "A-hole," she muttered in a soft voice as she moved to the other lane to let the truck pass. However, instead of zooming past her, the truck shifted into her lane.

"Ugh." Must be some drunk dude. She sped up to get away from the headlights, but the truck kept up.

The hairs on her arms stood on end, and her stomach tensed. *Oh God.* This wasn't some drunk asshole. Whoever it was, they were doing this deliberately.

Her heart beat like a timpani, ringing in her ears as she realized there was real danger here. She was still a few miles from her exit. What could she do? *Keep calm*, she told herself.

Georgina stepped on the gas, going ten miles over the speed limit. Her compact car shook from the acceleration and was no match for the truck as it caught up to her. The truck's monster engine roared, and she let out a scream as she lost control of the wheel and her car fishtailed across the concrete.

"Mommy!"

Grayson's voice cut into her gut like a knife, and the car jerked when she slammed on the brakes. They swerved off the highway, and wheels sprayed gravel all over the shoulder.

"Oh God! Grayson!" She turned around. He was secure in his car seat, but his eyes were wide open.

"Mommy! What happened?"

"I—" She looked outside. No sign of the truck. In fact, there was no one else on the highway. Reaching toward the back seat, she rubbed his leg. "Are you hurt baby? I'm so sorry. There was a … deer on the road and I didn't want to hurt it." No use alarming him. She wasn't even sure what that was about, though the tightening in her gut wasn't going away.

"I'm okay. I'm strong." He puffed up his cheeks. "I'm just glad we didn't hurt the deer. My new friend Kayla is a doe."

"Yeah, me too." She glanced around again. "Let's go home." As she reached for the gear shift, her hands began to shake. Her grip was so weak she could hardly move it. And, as she turned the key in the ignition, the engine remained silent. *Oh crud.* She hit her head on the steering wheel and let out a deep sigh. This was not what she needed right now.

"Mommy?" Grayson asked. "Whatsa matter?"

She cleared her throat. "Sorry, sweetie. Car trouble. Hold on, okay?" Stepping out of the car, she paced back and forth, trying to think of what to do now. If the car needed repairs, she'd be screwed because she didn't have much money left. But that wasn't her priority now. If that person who tried to get them off the road came back … no, they had to get out of here and get home first.

Georgina stared at her cell phone. In trying to save a buck, she didn't get the service membership with the twenty-four-hour emergency towing service. She didn't think she'd ever need it. *Darn.* Who could she call? She supposed she could call Kate or Sybil, but it was getting late and they lived in the opposite part of town. The only other people she really knew in Blackstone were Matthew and Jason. What else could she do? She swallowed a gulp and dialed her boss's number.

"Georgina?" came Matthew's voice through the receiver. "Is everything okay?"

"I … so sorry to call so late, but I'm in a bit of a bind." She quickly explained to Matthew what happened with "the deer."

"That's terrible," Matthew said. "Are you and Grayson okay? You're not hurt are you?"

"Yeah, we're fine. I just can't get the car to start." Georgina bit her lip. "Sorry, I didn't know who else to call. Do you happen to have the number of the garage in town? J.D.'s Garage? Kate took me there, but I can't find the number."

"I'll do you one better," Matthew said. "I'll send someone to come pick you up and take you home. Let me call Luke."

"What?" What was he saying? "You don't have to! I mean, sorry for the bother! I can call J.D.—hello? Matthew?" The line went dead. She gave the rear tire a kick. "Crap!"

"You said a bad word, Mommy!" Grayson said from inside the car.

Double crap. She walked around the rear passenger side, opened the door, and slid in next to Grayson. "Sorry. I'll put a dollar in the swear jar when we get home."

"Are we going to stay here all night, Mommy?" Grayson looked worried.

"Oh no. Uh, Luke is gonna come get us."

"Luke?" His eyes went wide.

"Yeah. Say," she reached for the light overhead and flipped it on, "why don't we do some drawing while we wait for him?" She put the activity tray over his car seat and grabbed the coloring books and crayons she kept in the back, setting them up for Grayson.

As she sat there, Georgina contemplated what had happened. Whoever tried to run them off the road did it on purpose. But why? Did The Chief find them? The thought made her blood freeze. But it wasn't like the last time they had been taken. For one thing, if The Chief wanted them back, they wouldn't be here waiting inside the car.

The truck just drove off. What was going on? Georgina racked her brain, trying to figure out the answers.

After twenty minutes, a pair of headlights coming up in the distance made Georgina look up. For a moment, fear gripped her. What if that truck was coming back? However, as the lights came closer, she saw the familiar sight of Luke's truck. She breathed a sigh.

The truck made a U-turn and stopped behind her car. She saw Luke get out of the truck and plod toward them.

"You okay?" he asked as he bent down to peer into the car window. "What happened?"

"Luke!" Grayson cried, waving his arms. "Mommy almost

hit a deer!"

Luke peered at her, a blond brow raised. She sucked in a breath. "I didn't want to hurt it."

"All right then. Why don't we get you into my truck and back home?"

"That would be great," she said. She felt vulnerable, being out here, knowing someone had tried to hurt her and Grayson. Despite her embarrassment at having Luke, of all people, come here to rescue them, his presence was oddly soothing.

She unbuckled Grayson and helped him, while Luke opened the door and grabbed the seat. After getting Grayson set up, they were on the way. They weren't too far away and were outside her door in less than fifteen minutes, which was a good thing because the ride was silent and uncomfortable.

"Thank you," she said as she unbuckled her belt. "I'll take him in." Except she was barely out the door and Luke was already taking Grayson out of his seat. She caught up to him outside her front door. "I said I'll take him in. You don't have to do that."

Grayson's arms were wrapped around his neck. "You're so tall, Luke!"

"Do you mind?" Luke said, looking at the door.

She shrugged and grabbed her keys, then opened her front door. He let her in first and followed behind her.

"Say goodnight to Luke and get ready for bed," Georgina said.

"Do I have to? Can Luke and I play in the backyard for a bit?" Grayson said with a big yawn.

"It's much too late for that, young man," Georgina said with a wag of her finger.

"Aw …" Grayson pouted and then wiggled out of Luke's

arms. "Can't you stay, Luke?"

"Luke's leaving," Georgina stated. "Now, scoot, young man! I'll come and tuck you in when you're dressed and ready, okay?"

"All right. G'night Luke!" Grayson said.

"Good night, Grayson," Luke replied. Grayson took off and disappeared down the hallway.

When Georgina was sure Grayson was far away enough so he wouldn't hear, she turned back to Luke. "Thank you again. I'm sorry about this whole thing. I told Matthew I just needed J.D.'s number and that he—"

"Why'd you call him?" Luke said.

"Huh?"

"I said, why did you call Matthew?" His jaw was tense as was his entire posture.

Her brows knitted together. "I didn't have anyone else to call."

"You have my number." He took a step forward and loomed over her.

She shrugged. "I didn't want to bother you."

"But you'd bother Matthew?"

"Yes, I—" She cleared her throat. He was so close to her, she felt tiny next to him. Was he trying to intimidate her? She squared her shoulders. "Why should I call you? You've made it crystal clear you don't want to be around me."

He frowned. "I have?"

"First, you didn't want me to cook you dinner. And then you didn't want to stay for coffee. I haven't even heard from you since then. You wouldn't even be here if Matthew didn't call you." She put her hands up. "It's all right, really. I know when I'm being a bother."

Luke's hands caught hers so quickly, she didn't even have

time to blink. "It's not what you think."

"It's not?"

"It's just ... I can't."

"Can't what?"

She let out a small squeak when Luke pulled her to him. There was no time to protest or say anything else as Luke's mouth devoured hers and his body crushed her to him.

The shock as their lips touched sent tingles across her skin. His demanding lips moved over hers in an expert caress, coaxing her mouth open. His beard tickled her, but it was much softer than she'd imagined. When his tongue touched hers, her knees went weak. He must have felt her body going limp because he slid his palms down her back, over her buttocks, and to her knees, then lifted her up off her feet.

Luke carried her over to the dining table, planting her on top, all the while not breaking the kiss. Damn, how could one man kiss so good? He moved between her legs, pressing his hips into hers. *Oh double-damn.* That was *not* a banana in his pocket. She raised her knees and wrapped her legs around him to pull him even closer.

His fingers dug into her hair, freeing it from the bun she usually wore. He groaned against her mouth, sucked on her bottom lip, then tugged at her scalp. *Triple-damn.* Her panties were soaked. She let out a moan and raked her fingers down his back.

Luke froze, which made her stop. He disentangled himself from her and stepped back. Wait, did she do something?

"Mommy, what are you doing on the table?"

Oh God. Grayson. "Umm, nothing," she said, sliding off the table and smoothing her hands down her blouse and pants. "I mean, there was, uh, a mouse. And I jumped up. On the table."

"And Luke's still here!" Grayson ran over to him. "I

thought you were leaving! Can you tuck me in, too?"

"Er, I think we should go to bed. Luke probably has places to go." Georgina quickly picked Grayson up and whisked him back to his room. She didn't know how it was possible, but her face still felt flush. Hopefully, Grayson didn't notice. It was a good thing Luke's super hearing picked up on him before he saw ... anything.

Grayson hopped in his bed, and Georgina arranged his blankets over him. He let out a yawn. "G'night, Mommy. See you in the morning."

"Good night, sweetie." She kissed him on the forehead, got up, and turned the lights off before leaving. When the door shut behind her, she let out a long sigh. The adrenaline—from the kiss and having Grayson walk in on them—rushed out of her body and left her drained so bad she had to brace herself against the wall.

She touched her lips, which felt branded even now. Luke kissed her. And she kissed him back. It really happened. He said he can't. Can't what? And what did this all mean? This was all so confusing. A good night's sleep might do the trick. How could she even sleep after that kiss?

Maybe an hour or two of TV might help. Some trashy reality show should keep her mind off things. When she walked out to the living room, however, she got the shock of her life.

"Luke?" He was standing in her living room, in the same spot she'd left him. "What are you still doing here?" She'd fully expected him to walk out and leave, like all the other times.

"I couldn't go."

"You couldn't?"

He shook his head and walked toward her. "Not without telling you something."

Her heartbeat sped up. "What's that?"

"You're not a bother," he said. "You could never be a bother to me."

"Luke—"

He silenced her with another kiss, one that was gentler. His hands cupped her jaw, tipping her face up to meet his. Firm lips moved over hers in a sweet caress, and when he pulled away, she was breathless.

"You owe me a dinner," was all he said.

She blinked. "I do?"

"You offered to cook me a thank you dinner," he reminded her. "I don't recall saying no."

"You didn't?"

"So, what time's good tomorrow?" he asked.

"Around seven?"

"Good. I'll be here." He pivoted on his heel and headed to the door.

Georgina watched, her body frozen. When the door closed, she staggered back against the dining room table.

Luke was coming over tomorrow. For dinner. Or was it a date? Would there be more kissing involved? On other furniture surfaces, she hoped. But Grayson would be here. Surely he expected him to be around. Should she make other arrangements? For a moment, she considered running after him to ask, but her legs weren't working. Oh God, this was too confusing. Maybe she should just tell him not to come. Sure, she was attracted to him, but what would become of this?

But she didn't want to cancel. She wanted to see him again and definitely kiss him again. And maybe even more.

Georgina sank down in a chair and then banged her head on the table. Good grief, why did this have to be so complicated?

CHAPTER EIGHT

As Luke walked back to his truck, his lion purred with pleasure. Now *that* was new. He huffed and got into his truck, then drove off.

He had tried to stay away from Georgina. Really, he had. She had enough going on and so did he. Christina said they were working on finding him answers about his pride, but they were still reading through all of Dr. Mendle's diaries. Apparently, there was over twenty years' worth of information they had to sift through.

He still kept going on his nightly patrols and tried to avoid going to their house. But his lion wouldn't let him sleep, not until it knew Georgina and Grayson were safe at home. But aside from that, he avoided her.

But then the call from Matthew came.

His animal went crazy, knowing they were stuck on the side of the road, alone and vulnerable. And of course, jealousy had reared its ugly head, which was fucking insane because Matthew would never cheat on Catherine. But it had stung, knowing she had called another man first and not him.

And then there was that kiss. He didn't know what had come over him, but when she said she was a bother to him, it had irked him. More than irked him, actually, and he wanted to show her she wasn't a bother.

That kiss had shaken him to the core, and in that moment, he was done. Done fighting with himself, his animal, with fate. Surely, if he was a terrible person and didn't deserve some happiness in this world, he never would have met Georgina. He was man enough to admit it scared the shit out of him—that something so good and pure was within arm's reach.

But there was also the possibility it could be taken away from him. Georgina could reject him and realize he wasn't worth it. He didn't want to bait-and-switch her, so he decided the only way to go was to come clean and if she didn't want any part of him, then he could at least have that definitive answer.

Tomorrow would be the day. *Dinner, at her place.* He frowned, realizing another factor. Grayson. While he enjoyed the boy's company, it was going to be difficult to talk to Georgina with him in the same room. An idea struck him.

He pulled over to the side of the road and took out his phone. Hopefully it wasn't too late.

"Hey, sorry, I know you're probably in bed by now, but I need a favor."

The next day after work, Luke took advantage of the employee shower facilities at the mines. After washing up, he got dressed in his best clothes. With a frown, he stared down at his red flannel shirt and least-faded pair of jeans. He only threw stuff out when it was falling apart and avoided shopping like the plague, but now he wished he had taken the time to find a new shirt at least.

After he finished, he drove to Georgina's and arrived there exactly five minutes before seven. As he pulled up in front of her house he saw a familiar silver Prius arrive at the same time. *Good.* She was here.

"Luke!" Sybil said in an excited voice as she exited her car and ran up to him. Much to his surprise, she threw herself into his arms and squeezed tight. "I'm so happy for you! It's her, right? She's the one? Georgina is your mate?"

"Yes." Sybil was smart, of course, and he knew she would figure it out. He had never asked her for a favor, after all. "But she doesn't know. Yet."

She ran her finger across her lips like she was closing a zipper. "Your secret's safe with me! Just go get your girl, okay?"

Hopefully, with Sybil's help, that was going to happen. "Thanks for coming on such short notice," he said as they walked up to the front door.

"For my brother," she chuckled and hugged his side, "I'd do anything."

Luke gave her hair an affectionate ruffle, then rang the doorbell. A few seconds later, the door opened.

"Luke." Her voice was low and breathy, sending desire straight to his cock. She looked beautiful, as she always did, but she definitely dressed up tonight. Her brown curls were carefully piled on top of her head, and though her red dress was modestly covering her shoulders, chest, and went down to her knees, the fabric clung to her every luscious curve.

He swallowed hard. "Georgina."

Georgina's gaze landed on Sybil. "Oh, hello Sybil."

"Hey, Georgina," Sybil greeted. "Guess what? I'm your babysitter for the night."

Georgina's face turned from confusion to surprise. "A babysitter?"

"Well, technically, I'll be taking Grayson out to the movies." She looked up at Luke, then back at Georgina. "If it's okay?"

She hesitated. "I don't know. We didn't really plan for this."

"I heard about what happened to Penny," Sybil began. "Don't worry, you know I'll be able to handle him."

"I guess, but—"

"Luke! Luke!" Grayson came running over to them. "You're here! Mommy said you were having dinner with us."

"Hello, Grayson," Sybil said, bending down to his level.

"You remember Sybil, don't you Grayson?"

"Hi, Miss Sybil," Grayson said in a shy voice.

Sybil chuckled. "Hey squirt. I think you should call me Auntie Sybil." She gave Luke a sly smile. "I mean, that's what you call Kate, right?"

"All right, Auntie Sybil."

"So, Grayson," Sybil began. "I have a problem I was hoping you could help me out with."

"What is it?"

"I really want to see that cartoon superhero movie that's out. Marvel Man."

His eyes went wide. "Marvel Man? I saw the trailer the other day! It looked so cool!"

"It just opened today and," she pulled out two pieces of paper from her pocket, "I scored these for tonight! You wouldn't happen to be interested—"

"Oh Mommy, can I go watch the movie with Auntie Sybil, please?" Grayson looked up at his mother with pleading eyes.

Georgina looked at Sybil. "If it's not too much trouble."

"It'll be awesome, right, squirt?" Sybil held up her hand and Grayson gave her a high-five. "And we can have hotdogs and popcorn for dinner." She winked at Grayson.

"Yay! I'll go get my shoes!" Grayson ran off, skipping happily as he disappeared into the house.

Georgina opened the door wider. "Let me get my purse and get you some money for the tickets and—"

"Nah, it's my treat," Sybil said, then let out a sigh. "To be honest, I really need tonight to just relax and not think about anything. Work's been hectic."

Grayson came back seconds later, his shoes on his feet and jacket in his hand. "Let's go Auntie Sybil! We can't miss the previews!"

Sybil laughed. "All right, squirt, hold your horses. Let's get you strapped in."

They transferred Grayson's car seat over to Sybil's car and secured the boy inside.

"Thanks, Sybbie," Luke said.

Georgina chuckled. "Sybbie?"

"Luke was about five or six when I was born," Sybil began as she walked over to the other side of her Prius. "Mom said he couldn't pronounce 'Sybil' so he would call me Sybbie. And the name stuck. Well," she slipped into the driver's seat, "we're off."

"Have fun!" Georgina leaned down and peered into the back seat. "Be good!"

Grayson waved his hand. "I will!"

As soon as they drove off, Georgina turned to Luke, hands on her hips. "That was rather sneaky," she said, an eyebrow raised.

"Should we call them back?" Luke asked.

"No!" She slapped a hand over her mouth. "I mean, let's go before dinner gets cold." She turned around and walked into the house.

Luke never thought he would find a woman adorable, but that's what Georgina was, especially when she got flustered. And it wasn't that he didn't notice how she acted around him; rather, he had chosen to ignore it, so wrapped up in himself. He also did not fail to notice how turned on she was last night and how her sweet scent wrapped around him as they made out on the dining table.

He wasn't planning on having sex tonight, no matter how much he wanted her. They would have to take things slow. He wasn't an expert on women, much less human women, but he knew he couldn't just jump into bed with her, not until she understood what she would be getting into.

Luke followed her into the kitchen, the smell of food wafting into his nose. It was delicious, but what made his mouth water was the sight of Georgina bent over, taking something out of the oven. Her shapely, pert ass pressed against the fabric of her dress, and his eyes traced her curves all the way down to her knees, calves, and ankles. Sex wasn't on the agenda, but that didn't mean they couldn't have a repeat performance of last night.

"Need help?" he asked, coming up behind her. He had to shove his hands into his pockets to keep them from touching her.

She stood up. "I'm good." She brought the tray with a roast chicken over to the dining room then laid it on the table. It was set for three people, and the potatoes and salad were already waiting. "Please," she motioned to the empty chair, "it's not fancy or anything. It was the fastest thing I knew to make that was fool proof."

"I'm sure it's delicious." He put the napkin over his lap.

She chuckled as she walked around to serve him the sides. "Just be glad you didn't try the first couple of times I made this. Or any meal."

"You learned to cook by yourself?" he asked. "Your mom didn't teach you?"

Her hands shook as she spooned the potatoes onto his plate. He caught her hand to steady it.

Georgina took a deep breath and pulled her hand away. "Uh, no," she said in a quiet voice, and then went back to her seat across from him.

Luke's gut twisted, seeing how her eyes suddenly dropped to her lap. He realized she'd never talked of her past, of what happened before they came to Dr. Mendle's lab. But Luke didn't care about that; maybe someday she'd be comfortable talking to him about the past, but all that mattered now was the future. "So," he said as he grabbed a piece of chicken and placed it on his plate. "Do you like working for Lennox?"

"Oh, it's fine," she said.

"I hope Matthew and Jason aren't working you too hard."

She gave a little laugh. "I can handle it. It was tough at first and it may not seem like it, but it's easy once you get to know both their routines and personalities."

He knew well enough how the two dragons could be different, despite their identical looks. "I imagine Matthew can be more demanding."

"That's because there's more pressure on him," she said. "But they're both fair bosses. And the benefits and being able to bring Grayson to the daycare without extra cost can't be beat. I used to spend half my paycheck just for a babysitter during the day while I was working."

"So you think you'll stay and work for them?"

She cleared her throat. "My, you're awfully chatty tonight," she remarked. "What about you? Do you like your work?"

"Can't complain." He took a bite of the chicken and swallowed. "It's good work and, like you said, the benefits from Lennox are great. I don't really need much to get by." Food, gas, and beer were all he needed. He had tucked away most of his salary from working at the mines; it wasn't millions, but it was more than most people had.

As they continued to chat and eat dinner, Luke couldn't help but be even more drawn to her. She seemed so animated when she talked, but it was the little details that caught his eye. Like the way her eyes sparkled when she laughed or her teeth sank into her lower lip when she was thinking of something. Of course, his enhanced hearing couldn't ignore the way her heart sped up when their hands accidentally brushed when he was passing her the salad. He didn't need a reminder that she wanted him too, but it was nice to know.

"Coffee?" she said as she stood up.

"Sure." After what had happened last time and how she thought he was brushing her off, he didn't want to say no to her offer of coffee. Hell, he probably wouldn't be able to say no to her ever again. "Maybe we should have coffee on the couch."

Despite her calm exterior, he saw the pulse in her throat jump. "Just black?"

"Yes."

He walked over and sat on the couch and waited for her. A few minutes later, she came out with two cups, set them on the coffee table, and sat next to him. He picked up the mug in front of him and took a sip.

"I like it with a little cream and sugar," she said. "But not all the time."

She was only a few inches away from him, and in the soft light of the living room, her skin seemed to glow and her eyes were like dark pools. It was intoxicating—her smell, her entire being. Luke knew he had to get a hold of himself or else he would lose control and scare her away.

He put down the mug, fully intending to calm himself enough to talk to her. "Georgina, I—" His back slammed against the couch as Georgina launched herself at him and pressed her mouth to his. This wasn't what he was expecting, but he'd take it.

As he kissed her back, his hands slid down to her waist and lower to cup her buttocks, then lifted her onto his lap. He could feel every curve of her delectable body pressed up against him as her weight settled on top of his. Fuck, every-thing about her was delicious, from the way her mouth tasted to the warmth emanating from between her thighs, and he was hard in an instant. He shifted his hips up so he could rub his cock against her. She mewled against his mouth and ground down hard on top of him.

Her hands slid up from his shoulders and into his hair. Fingers scraped against his scalp and tugged at his locks, a move that had him nearly creaming his pants like some inex-perienced teen. The smell of her arousal was making his brain go haywire, and he just had to touch her. He pulled her dress up to her waist, so she could straddle him, and dug his fingers into the soft flesh of her thighs.

She gasped as his erection pressed against her pussy through the thin fabric of her panties. He slipped his hand between her legs from behind, skimming his fingers over the damp cotton. Her body shuddered as he traced over her.

Fuck, he wanted her so bad. All he had to do was unzip his jeans and he could be inside her in seconds. Which was why it took all his might to pull away from her. "Georgina, we can't—"

"Oh!" she cried and scrambled off his lap. "Oh. God. I'm sorry, I don't know what came over me." She turned away from him and put her face in her hands, letting out a groan.

She was embarrassed, that was obvious. "Georgina, it's fine."

"I just thought you wanted to do that," she said. "I figured that was why you had Sybil come and take Grayson away."

"I did?"

She scooted away from him. "I'm sorry; I read things wrong. I thought you wanted—"

"Hold on." He moved closer to her, but she scurried farther away. As she got to the end of the couch, he placed a hand across her to bar her from getting up. "I do want you, Georgina. I thought that was pretty fucking obvious after last night."

Big brown eyes looked up at him. "You do? Then why did you pull away just now?"

"I want you, but I wanted to make sure you knew what you were getting into before we jump into bed."

"Oh." Her shoulders relaxed, and she shook her head. "I don't know how to do this anymore. It's been so long since ...."

"I don't either." When her eyebrow shot up, he gave a small laugh. "I'm not inexperienced, but this," he took her hand, so small and delicate in his big, rough palms, and kissed her fingers, "I'm no good at this." When she tried to protest, he held up a hand. "I'm broken, and I don't know if I'm good for you."

"Luke ...." She placed a hand on his cheek.

He wanted her to understand. But where to start?

From the beginning, he guessed. "When Hank and Riva took me in, they didn't know I'd turn into such a monster."

"You're not—"

He turned his head and kissed her palm. "Let me finish. My animal broke that day they found me. Or it was already broken long before that, who knows? Hank was strong enough to keep me reined in. Until one day, he just couldn't." He took a deep breath, his stomach clenching at the thought of her knowing what he had done. How he tore their family apart. But she had to know.

Slowly, he told her every bit, every detail. He didn't make excuses; he had none, after all. He was afraid of her reaction, imagining the look of disdain on her face. It was his biggest fear; she was a mother and if Grayson ever told her what he had said to Riva, she would be devastated, too.

But he was surprised by what he saw when he had scrounged up the courage to look at her—tears forming in her eyes as she reached for him. "Luke, I'm sorry."

"I'll understand if you want me to go and never want to see me again." His chest tightened at those words.

"No, I don't want that." She placed both her hands on his jaw and moved her face up to kiss him. "You were young, and you said and did something stupid. I remember what that was like." She scoffed. "People you're related to by blood aren't always any better."

"She'll never forgive me." And that was the truth he had always been afraid to say.

"What? She's your mother, Luke, she'll forgive you, if you ask."

It was nice of her to say, but he knew it wasn't true. What he had done was unforgivable. He tried to turn away from her, so she couldn't see the shame on his face, but she refused to let him, holding firmly onto his jaw.

"Luke," she said. "Look at me. I don't care about that. I mean, I do because I know it's hurting you and your family, but I still think you're a good guy and ... I like you. A lot." She smiled. "Like, *a lot*." She kissed him square on the mouth. "And I want you too, Luke."

He let out the breath he'd been holding. She said those words, but he still couldn't quite believe it. "I promise you'll only get the best parts of me. Not the broken pieces."

"I want all of you," she declared, looking straight into his eyes. "Every part. Even the broken pieces because that's all you."

God, he didn't deserve her. She didn't even know what she was getting into. "We need to take things slow."

She sighed. "You're right. It's complicated with Grayson and everything."

"I don't want to confuse him, especially with what happened to you." She nodded in agreement. "But I'd like to spend more time with you. Both of you."

"You don't mind?" she asked in a small voice. "The baggage I have?"

"He's not baggage," he said. "He's your everything. I get that. Which is why we need to take our time."

"I'm sorry I jumped all over you." Her cheeks turned red.

He chuckled. "Don't be sorry." He gathered her into his arms. "I want it to happen and it's taking every Goddamn ounce of my strength not to rip this dress off you." He gave her a kiss on the forehead. "There's something else you need to know."

"There is?"

"Yes. I'll tell you when the time is right." It was too much tonight, after everything he'd said. He was afraid she'd run in the other direction if she knew how devoted to her he already was.

"We don't have to jump into bed or anything, but the other stuff … was nice," she said in a low, sultry voice.

He buried his nose in her hair. "I could definitely do other *stuff.*" She let out a laugh when he hauled her onto his lap again.

"What time does that movie end?" she asked.

He gave an annoyed snort and checked the time. "Probably not long enough." Sybil warned him it wasn't a long movie, and he guessed they'd be back soon.

"We'll make do with what time we have."

Luke slid his fingers behind her head again and pulled her down for a kiss. He didn't know how, but he swore she tasted sweeter each time he kissed her. Her mouth opened to him, and their tongues danced as they touched.

He moved his hands up to cup her full breasts through her dress. She moaned and pressed down against him, her knees parting to straddle him. He could smell how aroused she was, if the fact that she was grinding down on his cock wasn't obvious enough.

She threw her head back and shuddered. Her scent flooded his nostrils. He clamped his lips on her neck, right on the sweet spot under her ear, sucking on the soft flesh.

"Luke!" Her hands dug into his hair; she tangled her fingers as she pulled and her body shuddered. Fuck, the friction was too much, and his cock was leaking with pre-cum, soaking his underwear.

He moved a hand behind her again, lifting her dress up so he could slip his fingers into her panties. She was Goddamn dripping onto his fingers, and when he pushed a finger inside her pussy, she let out a loud cry.

"Ffuuck," he muttered through clenched teeth. He leaned back and watched her grinding on top of him, her teeth biting into her lower lip and her eyes closed. He lifted his hips off the couch, his cock seeking out the heat and friction between her legs.

"Luke, I'm—" She cried out, her fingers clutching at his shoulders as her body shook. Even through the layers of clothing, he could feel her pulse and throb as she came. He gritted his teeth and closed his eyes, his control thread-thin.

Her breathing slowed down, and she fell against him. He rubbed his palms down her back in a soothing manner. A few seconds passed, and she looked up at him, her cheeks pink and an embarrassed smile on her face.

"It's been a while," she said. "I got a little carried away."

He pushed a lock of hair out of her eyes. "I like it when you get carried away."

She moved her hands down his chest, and lower still, over his abdomen. "How about I—"

The sound of the doorbell made them pull away from each other. Luke adjusted the front of his jeans as Georgina sprang to her feet and smoothed down her dress. She walked over to the front door and opened it.

"How was the movie?" she asked as Grayson and Sybil walked inside.

"It. Was. Awesome!" He raised a fist in the air. "First there was this explosion that turned Jack Lee into Marvel Man! And then later the aliens came! Then boom! Marvel Man saves the world!"

"Sounds like a fun movie," Georgina said. "Did you behave for Auntie Sybil?"

"He was a complete angel," Sybil answered, giving Grayson a wink. "Right squirt?"

He winked back. "Right."

"Well, it's almost your bedtime," Georgina said. "Why don't you say good night and thank you to Sybil."

"Thank you, Auntie Sybil," Grayson said.

Sybil bent down and opened her arms, and the little boy eagerly hugged her. "Thank you, squirt," she said. "Maybe we can do it again." She gave Georgina a wink. "I'd be happy to babysit *any* time."

"Good night, Luke," Grayson said.

"'Night." When Grayson wrapped his small arms around Luke's legs, he patted his head.

"Go and get ready for bed," Georgina instructed. With a last wave, Grayson ran out of the living room.

"I really appreciate you taking him to the movies," Georgina said to Sybil. "I've been meaning to do something with him; I just never have the time or chance."

"My pleasure. Really, it was the best date I've had in years," Sybil joked. "I know pathetic, right? Anyway," she looked meaningfully at Luke and then back to Georgina, "I hope dinner was good?"

When Georgina turned beet red, Luke cleared his throat. "I'll walk you to your car, Sybbie, if you don't mind waiting for a sec."

"Sure, I'll just be outside."

As soon as Sybil left, he turned back to Georgina. "Should I come by tomorrow? Maybe you, me, and Grayson can go downtown for lunch. Then to the park?"

"That sounds great," she said. "I'll see you then."

He leaned down and brushed his lips against hers. "I'll see you at eleven." Luke walked out the door and closed it behind him. When he got outside, he rolled his eyes as Sybil stood on the stoop, her hands over her mouth as she danced excitedly.

"Ohmigod, ohmigod, ohmigod! Is it done? Are you mates yet?" she asked.

He chuckled. "No." *Not yet*, he thought, and his lion roared with pleasure.

"But … you guys are good, right?"

"Yeah," he said with one last glance at the door. "We're good."

CHAPTER NINE

GEORGINA SLEPT like a baby last night. Why wouldn't she? After such a delicious orgasm, anyone would sleep soundly and with a smile the size of Texas on their face. She still blushed, thinking about it this morning as she cleaned up last night's dishes in the kitchen.

Luke wanted her. Hell, he *liked* her. He didn't see her as some pest. Well, that was pretty obvious based on how he touched her and that sizable bulge in his pants last night.

Oh God, could she really do this? It wasn't just going to be sex, that was clear to her. Even now, her heart was hammering, thinking about it.

And then there was that itch, scratching at her brain. *You know you can't stay,* a voice inside her said. *You know what you are. And if he found out—*

The sound of the glass breaking as it hit the floor made her jump. She winced in pain as she bent down to remove the small shard that got stuck in her foot. "Darnit!"

Georgina hopped over to one of the chairs by the kitchen

table, grabbing a clean rag to wrap around the wound. She winced as she pressed down, hoping to stop the flow of blood.

She sighed and planted her face in her free hand. Luke had told her his truth, wanting to come clean with her. Frankly, she thought it would be worse. And she did mean what she had said. She knew if Riva loved him like a son, nothing would ever take that away. Grayson could tell her a hundred times she wasn't his mom and it would never be true in her heart.

But, if Luke knew *her* truth, would he be able to overlook it?

"It's not my fault." She pressed her hand over her foot so hard, her knuckles went bone white. *I didn't choose it. Any of it.* Luke had been taken in by a kind and loving family, while she had been born into one that only knew hate.

The sharp rapping at the back door yanked her back to reality. *Who could it be this early on a Saturday?* She hopped over to the door and peeked out through the glass, pulling the door open as soon as she saw who it was.

"Luke?"

"Hi," he said, the corners of his mouth turning up into … a smile? Had she ever seen him smile like that? Or at all? It made him look even more handsome. "I thought I'd bring breakfast." He held up a large brown paper bag. "Is Grayson —" A familiar frown settled onto his face, and his gaze went down to her foot. "What the hell happened?"

"What? Oh—" She shrugged. "I dropped a glass while I was cleaning—Hey!" She yelped in surprise when she felt her feet lift off the floor. Luke wrapped one massive arm around her waist and carried her over to the kitchen counter.

He planted her on the granite top. "First aid kit?"

"On your left, second shelf."

She watched him as he turned around to reach for the kit inside her cabinet. *Grrr, how could one man look so sexy, even from behind?* His back muscles rippled under the tight shirt he wore, and the way his jeans clung to his ass should be illegal.

Luke turned back, first aid kit in hand, and knelt down in front of her. He carefully cleaned the wound with an antiseptic wipe, checking her foot for any more glass shards before placing a plastic bandage over it. As he got up, his hands traced up her calves and thighs before settling on her waist. "You should really be more careful," he said, his golden eyes staring right into her.

She couldn't hold back her shiver, especially as his fingers played with the hem of her shirt. Though she was wearing a shirt and sleep shorts, she might as well have been naked, the way he was looking at her.

He moved closer, nudging her knees open so he could stand between her thighs. A hand slid up the side of her face and cradled her jaw. Her heart raced as he leaned down—

"Mommy? Luke?"

He practically leapt away from her when Grayson walked into the kitchen, rubbing his eyes sleepily.

Grayson let out a yawn. "What are you doing here?" He looked at Georgina on top of the counter. "Is there another mouse?"

Oh dear. "No, sweetie. I hurt my foot and Luke was helping me." She wiggled her foot at him, showing him the plastic bandage. "See?"

"Oh Mommy, you have a booboo?" He walked over to her and peered at her foot. "Did Luke kiss it to make it all better?"

Luke coughed, and Georgina couldn't help but smile. "Er, yes, he made it all better."

"I brought breakfast. From Rosie's," Luke said, clearing his throat. "Fresh made pastries. They're the best."

"Wow!" Grayson's eyes went wide, and he sniffed the air. "Smells yummy!"

"Uh, have you gone potty yet?" He shook his head. "Go on then. We'll wait for you to start."

The little boy nodded eagerly and then ran off. She turned to Luke. "What are you doing here? I mean, I know you brought breakfast, but I thought you said you'd be by at eleven?"

"I couldn't wait to see you again," he said, moving back to stand between her thighs. "And I was thinking, there are a couple of things I could do around here before we go."

"Things? Like what?"

"Well, I noticed your gutters haven't been cleaned. You gotta do that before the rains come. And there's a board on your porch that's loose. I don't want you or Grayson tripping on that."

She laughed. "My landlord can get that taken care of! It's his—"

He interrupted her with a quick kiss. "I know, but I want to," he whispered against her mouth. "I need to."

Need? Why would he need to fix my porch and— "Hmmm …." Oh, damn him and his kisses. She forgot what she wanted to say as soon as his warm lips touched hers. The kiss only lasted seconds before he pulled away, but Georgina felt like someone had squeezed all the air out of her.

"Why don't you put those pastries on a plate and get a pot of coffee brewing while I clean up?" He nodded to the broken glass on the floor.

"O-okay." She hopped off the counter and grabbed some plates from the cupboard.

As she prepared breakfast, she couldn't help but smile as she glanced over at Luke. He had found the broom in the utility closet and was carefully sweeping up the broken glass, going over the area twice and then once more with a wet rag to make sure he picked up every bit of glass.

Soon, the coffee was ready and the pastries were laid out on plates. Grayson had also come back to the kitchen just in time.

"I'm so hungry!" He took a deep breath. "That smells sooo good!"

"Have a seat," she instructed. Luke was already seated in one of the chairs around the kitchen table, and Grayson sat on the empty one next to him.

"Thank you for bringing us breakfast," she said to Luke.

"It's delicious!" Grayson said through a mouthful of danish, his face already covered with jam and flaky crumbs.

"Not a problem," he said as he bit into the croissant she put on his plate.

Georgina took a sip of her coffee and closed her eyes. She was almost afraid to open them again and wake up and realize this was all a dream. But it wasn't. This was *real*.

Grayson was babbling about the movie, and Luke listened intently, filling up his glass of milk and placing a chocolate pastry on his empty plate while nodding and asking questions.

Her heart clenched at the sight, and she pushed away all doubts in her mind.

After Luke had finished all the chores he wanted to do, plus mowed their lawn and threw out some junk in the garage she'd been meaning to get rid of, they all rode together to Main Street for lunch. Since they already had Rosie's pastries for breakfast, Luke suggested they go to the Italian place. Georgina thought it was way too fancy, especially with Grayson, but he insisted and assured her it was more casual than it looked.

The owner, Giorgio Allementari, seemed surprised to see Luke, commenting how it's been years since he'd been there. He also fawned over Georgina and Grayson and led them to the "usual table." Georgina looked to Luke for an explanation, but he didn't offer one. They followed Giorgio to the semi-circular booth in a corner of the restaurant.

The flamboyant restaurateur placed the menus on the table. "You aren't allergic to strawberries, by chance, are you *signorina*? Or gluten? Nuts? Dairy?"

"Uh, no," she said with a shake of her head.

He sighed with relief. "Good. I'll be back with your bread."

"Everything's good here," Luke said as he opened the menu. "Order what you want."

"I will," Georgina said. "And I'm paying."

"No—"

"Nuh-uh." She shook her head. "You've given me so much free labor today. The landlord said to take off what it cost me to get those repairs done, so you're saving me rent money this month."

He gave her another smile. "You have two shifters here, so I hope you won't regret it."

She laughed.

This was the first time she had taken Grayson anywhere more fancy than a diner or Rosie's, but she was glad Luke was there to show him how to hold his knife and put his napkin on his lap. Despite his rough exterior, Luke had the manners of a prince, which told her a lot about how he was raised. She wondered what she would say if she ever got to meet Riva Lennox.

After lunch, Luke suggested they walk around Main Street for some shopping and then he would take them to the park. They walked into a couple of stores, and it was nice that Luke could watch Grayson while she looked around. Normally, if she even had money to shop anywhere, she couldn't take more than five minutes before Grayson got bored.

Georgina didn't take too long, and she mostly enjoyed having time to herself as she browsed through the shops. She didn't want to torture the two boys (though they seemed happy enough, walking around the bookstore) so she told them she was done and that they could head to the park.

"Can I go on the swings? Please, Mommy?" Grayson pleaded as they strolled over to the playground. "And the jungle gym? And the slides? And the bars—"

"Of course," she said with a laugh. "You can go anywhere you want."

Georgina and Luke accompanied Grayson as he tested every piece of play equipment in the park. They pushed him on the swings, hoisted him up on the monkey bars, and spun him around the Merry-Go-Round. By the time he had gone around twice, Georgina's shirt was sticking to her skin, her brow was covered in sweat.

"Why don't you go take a break?" Luke suggested. "You look tired."

"I'm fine," she insisted, her breath coming in pants.

"There's no way he's going to stop." He nodded to Grayson, who was making quick work of the monkey bars. "Go and get a drink or something."

"I guess I could use some water." She was tired and sweaty.

Oh God, she probably looked terrible. Not that Luke was the type of guy who would notice. But still, she should probably go splash some water on her face and clean up. "I'm gonna go to the ladies' room first." She nodded toward the small bungalow in the middle of the park, marked with signs for the male and female restrooms. "I'll be back."

"We'll be here."

Georgina took one last glance at Grayson and waved at him before turning her back and heading toward the restroom. When was the last time she had felt this carefree? Or even seen Grayson so happy? Not in a long while. Maybe staying in Blackstone had been good for him. Maybe, just maybe—

The thought cut off as she tried to scream, but the hand over her mouth muffled any sound that came out. An arm snaked around her waist and pulled so hard all the air was knocked out of her. She found herself being dragged into the ladies' room, the door slamming loudly behind her.

"I'm gonna take my hand off, and you're not going to make any sound. No screaming, no calling for help. If you do, your boy is dead." The familiar voice made her blood freeze in her veins. "Nod if you understand."

Georgina knew it wasn't an empty threat, so she nodded. When he let her go, she took a deep breath and braced herself against the wall to keep herself from collapsing on the floor. "How … how did you find me?" she managed to choke out.

"Oh, you know I'll always find you, Georgie."

Oh God, how she hated that name he called her. It never failed to make her skin crawl. Slowly, she lifted her head, daring to face her attacker.

It had been five years since she last saw him, but he looked exactly the same. White hair buzzed close to his scalp. Weathered, scarred face. Usually, he wore fatigues and tight shirts that showed off his muscled body, but today, he looked more discreet in jeans and a button-down. Like he wanted to blend in.

"What do you want, Adrian?"

Adrian Vaughn, The Chief's right hand man, spat on the floor. "Once upon a time, you knew exactly what I wanted." She shuddered when he turned those cold dead eyes at her. "We had plans for you, Georgie. Me and The Chief. But you ruined everything by whoring yourself out to that animal!"

"I never would have agreed to marry you!" Adrian was nearly thirty years her senior, not to mention a sick bastard. The moment she turned eighteen, he didn't even bother to hide the lecherous looks. He and The Chief had apparently been scheming behind her back to force her to marry him.

"And then you got yourself pregnant!" He grabbed her by the collar and hauled her to her feet. "I wouldn't marry you even if you begged me! Not when you've spawned that abomination!"

"Are you going to punish me? Bring me back to The Chief?" she shouted at him. "Take me away and do what you want. J-just get it over with!"

He let out a cruel laugh. "Oh no, Georgie, you're not going anywhere."

"I-I'm not?"

"You're not getting off that easy. Besides, you're much more valuable to us now."

"I don't have a lot of money!" She tried to get away from him, but his grip tightened. "But you can have it all."

"We don't need your money," he said.

"Then let's go! Take me away, you don't even need to tie me up and gag me like last time."

He laughed. "Georgie, you know if The Chief wanted you back, you'd be on your way to HQ by now. Heck, we'd have taken you the other night after we spooked you in your car. *That* was just a warning."

"What do you want, then?" Oh God, please, don't let them be after Grayson.

"The Chief has big plans for you, now that you're working closely within Lennox. With your position, you can do so much more for us."

"Never!" She knew what he was saying. What he was asking. After all, she knew exactly how they operated. "I would never betray Matthew and Jason!"

"Have you forgotten who you are, Georgie?"

"Shut up!"

"If you don't do as we say, then you know what we'll have to do. Not only will we kill that boy of yours, but we'll tell your new friends who you *really* are!"

"No!" He can't. They could never know. *Oh God.* Luke could never find out. Not this way.

His face twisted into a cruel smile. "What do you think they would do if they found out you were The Chief's *daughter*?"

"You can't." She already sounded broken with her secret laid out. All these years, when she never said it out loud, it was like it wasn't real. But now, it was staring her right in the face.

"We will." Adrian grabbed her hand and placed something in it. "Here. Just put this into Jason Lennox's computer when you go back to work on Monday. You've got until noon."

She stared into her hand. It was a small USB drive. "What is it?"

"What does it matter?" he said. "Just do as we say. Or else."

"You'll never get away with this!"

"Ha! And who's going to stop us? The lion that's been sniffing around you? I already tangled with the Blackstone dragon back in London and lived. Luke Lennox is no match for me."

How the hell did he—Why did she bother wondering? Of course Adrian and The Chief would know. They knew *everything*.

Adrian continued. "I've got two snipers a hundred yards away. One word from me and your boyfriend and son get a bullet in their heads."

Her lower lip trembled as she imagined it happening—Luke and Grayson on the ground. Blood pooling around them.

"We'll know the exact moment you finish the job," Adrian said. "Or when you don't. So don't even think of running away until it's done." He narrowed his eyes at her.

"And after I'm done … what happens? What do I do?"

"I don't really give a damn. And it won't matter anyway, but," he looked her up and down, "I suppose if you needed protection of any sort, I could be persuaded—"

"Fuck off!" No way. She would rather rip her skin off than marry him.

He spat on the floor. "Uptight bitch. You think I'd even touch you after you've been with one of them? Or is it two now? More?"

"Get out!" She pushed at him, but he caught her hands.

"Such a waste." He let go of her as she tried to pull away, causing her to slam back into the wall. "Remember what I said, Georgie. Monday. Noon. And, until you finish the job, you act normal. Don't even think of running away from Blackstone, getting yourself fired from your job, or even breaking up with your boyfriend to save him. We've got eyes on you. We know where you live."

She stood there frozen, watching as Adrian turned to the door and then left. It took her a few seconds, but she finally started breathing again.

Oh God. She leaned her head against the wall. No, no, no. This couldn't be happening. Not now.

What was she supposed to do? If she explained everything to Matthew and Jason, would they even understand? And Luke. How could she even face him now?

She didn't know what was worse, them finding out about who she really was or having to face The Chief again.

Georgina straightened her shoulders. *No, the only thing worse was if Grayson got killed.* He was her priority, she always knew that. Protecting Grayson from The Chief and from anyone who tried to hurt him was her only concern.

She looked down at the USB drive in her hand. No biggie, right? All she had to do was slip it into Jason's computer. No one would even know it was her. Her gut tightened, but she ignored it.

Georgina walked over to the sink and splashed water on her face. Yes, no one would ever need to know it was her. And Grayson and Luke would be safe.

But, as she walked back outside to where Luke and Grayson were playing on the swings, a pain stabbed at her heart. Grayson was laughing and cheering as Luke pushed him higher and higher.

She was an idiot to think it would ever work out between them. He was a shifter and she was the daughter of one of the worst human beings in the world, one whose mission was to wipe out his kind. Even if she explained her side, he would never believe her. Why she even let herself get this far, she didn't know.

As she came closer to them, her body tensed and a bead of sweat ran down her temple. *Act normal*, Adrian had said. He was probably watching right now. If she did anything unusual, he'd see it. And he would kill Luke and Grayson on the spot. A high caliber bullet to the brain was one of the few things that could instantly kill most shifters. It was a painful lesson The Chief had taught her.

"Hey." Luke frowned. "You okay?"

"Me? Yeah, I'm fine." She fanned herself with her hand, trying to act casual. "God, it's sweltering out here."

"Yeah, maybe we should get going." He turned to where Grayson was playing by the slides and let out a whistle. "Grayson! Time to go!"

"Aww!" Grayson pouted. "Just five more minutes! Please, Luke?"

He turned to Georgina, and she shrugged. "Okay, five minutes but not a second more, ya hear?" Grayson let out a cheer of delight.

Luke sucked in a breath. "Actually, I was hoping for a couple of minutes alone with you. I need to talk to you."

"You do?" Oh God, he knew didn't he? He saw Adrian coming out of the ladies' room. She flinched inwardly, waiting for the hammer to drop.

"Yeah. I just got a call from Matthew."

"And?" she managed to squeak out, despite her throat being as dry as the Sahara.

"He wants me to come to dinner tomorrow night. At the castle. He says it's important, and he has an announcement to make."

"Oh." She wrinkled her brow. "That's fine. I mean, we don't have to spend every day together—"

"No, that's not it."

Luke scratched at the back of his head and shuffled his feet. *Wait, was he ... nervous?* "Luke?"

"Matthew said I should bring you and Grayson."

"He did? Why? Does he know about us?"

"I didn't tell him," he said. "But he knew about me coming over last week to help Grayson, and then Sybil told him about babysitting last night. So, let's assume everyone knows."

Oh crap.

"I'm sorry," he said in a sheepish voice. "Not that I didn't want anyone to find out about us spending time together, but I wasn't sure if you did."

"What? No, it's fine!" Her stomach twisted into knots, and Adrian's warning rang in her head. She had to act like everything was normal. "I mean, I'm sure Grayson would love to see the castle again."

He grabbed her hand and held it in his. "I haven't had dinner at the castle in a long time. I couldn't. I wanted to say no, but this felt important. To have you and Grayson there."

She sucked in a breath, hoping that would be enough to hold back the tears burning in her throat. "Of course. We'll be there."

He sighed in relief. "Let me go get Grayson. We can head over to the diner, and then I'll take you guys home."

She nodded and watched as Luke walked to the monkey bars and grabbed Grayson. Her son let out a high-pitched squeal as Luke flipped him over and placed him on his shoulders. It was too much, and she turned away.

The dread creeping into her chest grew heavier and heavier. How could she even keep it together tomorrow when she faced all his family and friends?

Maybe there was one bright side to this. Perhaps her betrayal would bring Luke back to his family. If anything, she gave a silent promise to do her best to mend the rift, while she still could.

CHAPTER TEN

FEW THINGS MADE LUKE NERVOUS. Sure, his lion paced and became edgy when there was danger or he was agitated, but his human side remained cool and calm, never reacting to the people and situations around him. Now, his palms were sweaty and his chest felt hollow, just thinking of being back at the castle. He'd been there a handful of times over the last few years, but he'd never felt this way.

Still, he didn't even think he'd feel anything ever again. Not until Georgina.

His lion wanted to claim her and make her theirs. But he didn't know the first thing about mates or how the mating process worked. Hank had tried to explain it to his kids when they were younger, but didn't really give them any details. "You'll know it when it happens," he had said. Luke wasn't even sure if that applied to him. Did it work the same way for lions as it did for dragons?

Maybe he should ask Matthew. The dragon shifter sounded both surprised and elated when Luke told him he was coming to dinner and bringing Georgina and Grayson. "I'm really glad you decided to come," Matthew had said. "It means a lot to me."

Luke already had a gut feeling of what this was about. And if he was right, he was happy for Matthew and Catherine. They'd probably been trying for a kid since they got married, and another Lennox dragon would be a welcome addition to the family.

The thought of having dinner at the castle created mixed feelings in him. Sure, he'd been there for Matthew's engagement party and wedding, but it was far from an intimate family dinner. He hadn't even set foot in the upper floors of the castle in years, much less sat in the family dining room in the east wing.

"You seem more anxious than me," Georgina observed, breaking his reverie. Her hands were wringing in her lap, but she looked at him with concern.

"You'll be fine," he said as he pulled his truck into Blackstone Castle's driveway. As he promised last night, he picked them up at home and they all drove up to the castle together.

"And you?" she asked, the corner of her lips turning up. "Will you be fine?"

He chuckled and slipped out of the driver's seat. "You and Grayson are here, so yes."

She gave him a smile, but one that didn't seem to reach her eyes. There was something about the expression on her face that didn't feel right to him. Georgina seemed skittish tonight, but he chalked it up to nerves. He hoped she could be comfortable around him first before he told her they were mates.

"Luke! Luke!" Grayson called from the back seat. "Don't forget me!"

"Oops, sorry, bud," he said as he opened the door and released Grayson from the car seat. The little boy jumped into his arms, and he set him down on the ground. "Let's go."

They walked up the driveway together, Georgina's hand in his while Grayson clung to the other. Luke rang the doorbell when they arrived at the front door.

"Good evening—Lucas?" The older man looked startled for a moment when his eyes fixed on Luke.

"Hello, Christopher," he said, greeting the Lennox's long-time butler. Christopher looked the same as he always did—clean and pressed white shirt and black pants, shoes polished to a shine. Hank and Riva didn't want things to be too formal around the castle, unlike in the old days, so they didn't require Christopher or any of the staff to wear uniforms or even coats. However, Christopher was still old school and liked to look presentable, even on normal days. This was about as casual as he got.

"Matthew said you'd be coming, but I didn't expect—" He cleared his throat and looked toward Georgina. "And you've brought Ms. Georgina and Grayson."

"Hello, Christopher," Georgina greeted.

Grayson, waved at the older man. "Heya, Christopher! How's butlering?"

Georgina laughed when Luke raised a brow at the boy. "When we were staying here, Grayson asked what Christopher did. He said he was a butler and so now Grayson calls his job 'butlering.'"

"Sounds important, taking care of everyone," Grayson added.

"It is," Luke said, giving a meaningful look at Christopher. He and his wife, Meg, had devoted their entire lives to Hank and Riva, and then their children. They would do anything for the Lennoxes, and he knew his family would do anything for the couple as well.

"Almost everyone is here," Christopher said. "They're upstairs in the east wing dining room."

"Thanks, Christopher."

Luke led Georgina and Grayson up the grand staircase and into the east side of the castle. Even though he hadn't been here in years, it still looked the same. The memories from his childhood suddenly flooded his mind—running down the halls with Jason and Matthew, playing hide and seek with Sybil, numerous birthday parties, Riva chasing after him when he didn't want to take a bath. It was like they happened a million years ago, yet being here again, the memories became crystal clear.

"Well, look who's here," Matthew said when they entered the dining room. He walked over to them from where he was standing in the corner with Ben, Penny, Catherine, Kate, and Sybil, then clapped him on the shoulder. "Glad you could make it." He turned to Georgina and Grayson. "You guys, too," he said with a warm smile.

"Thanks for inviting us," Georgina said.

"How could I not?" Luke shot him a warning look and Matthew cleared his throat. "I mean, I did tell Grayson he can come visit and explore anytime." He ruffled the boy's hair affectionately.

"Where are Jason and Christina?" Luke asked, glancing around.

"They're not sure they can make it. *Work stuff,*" Matthew said with a meaningful look. "But they said to go ahead without them if they don't get here by seven thirty. Can I get you guys some drinks? Beer for you, Luke? How about you, Georgina? And Grayson."

"Just water for me and maybe juice for Grayson?"

Matthew nodded. "Coming right up. Go ahead and join everyone. Meg just brought out some snacks."

As they walked over to where everyone was, Luke could sense the apprehension in Georgina. He guessed she was nervous, coming here with him. "You're fine," he said, placing a hand on the small of her back. She stiffened but nodded.

"Georgina! Grayson!" Kate greeted. "A little birdie told me you might be here!"

Sybil elbowed her. "Yeah, that was me. Hey, squirt!" She knelt down and drew in Grayson for a hug. "How're you doing?"

"I'm good, Auntie Sybil," he said.

"Hey!" Kate knelt down beside them. "Don't *I* get a hug?"

Ben laughed and slapped Luke on the shoulder. "You might need a shotgun to keep all the girls away when he grows up."

Luke hoped Georgina didn't hear that. She seemed stressed enough tonight. "Are we going to eat soon?"

"Yes," Catherine said. "Meg's almost done with the prep. Christina just messaged me; she said we should definitely start without them."

"We can start with the reason we called you here." Matthew slipped an arm around Catherine's waist, his hand going over her belly.

Sybil slapped a hand over her mouth. "Is it—"

Kate pointed to the sparkling water Catherine was drinking. "Oh. My. God. You're—"

"Pregnant?" Penny blurted out.

Catherine smiled. "Yes."

Cheers erupted from the girls, while Ben and Luke both clapped hands with Matthew and gave him hugs.

"This is great," Ben said. "Us becoming fathers at the same time. I was just telling Penny it'd be nice if our kid had cousins growing up, just like I did."

"We didn't want to tell anyone until after six weeks," Catherine said. "I did tell Chrissy as soon as I suspected, but made her promise not to tell anyone, not even Jason."

"He guessed it anyway," Matthew said with a chuckle. "It's hard to keep things from your twin."

"Congratulations, guys," Georgina said as she hugged Catherine. "I knew it would happen eventually."

"Thank you," Catherine said. "I'm so happy to be sharing this news with you all. We're going to video conference with Riva and Hank tonight as soon as they wake up in their time zone."

"Mom and Dad'll be over the moon!" Sybil cried.

"Mommy, when do we get to eat?" Grayson stage whispered to Georgina, who turned bright red.

"Grayson!" she admonished.

Matthew laughed. "I remember what it was like," he said. "C'mon. Meg cooked up a feast for all of us. And she made a chocolate cake for dessert."

They all sat down around the table, with Matthew at the head and Catherine on his right. Luke sat down on the left side, with Georgina beside him and Grayson next to her.

Dinner, as usual, was fantastic. When Meg came out and saw Luke, she was startled, much like her husband Christopher had been, but she went over to him and gave him a hug. She looked meaningfully at Georgina (because of course the sly old woman probably knew something was up) and whispered to him that she hoped he would be by more often. He didn't answer her, but instead, gave her hand a squeeze.

"I can't believe you got to eat this everyday while you were growing up," Penny said as she polished off the last bite of chocolate cake. "How do you all stay so fit?"

"Shifter metabolism," Matthew and Sybil said at the same time.

"Right," Penny chuckled and rubbed her stomach. "I better prepare myself."

"Stock up on everything," Georgina warned her and glanced over at Grayson, who was having his second slice of cake. "But it's all worth it."

Soon, the evening was winding down and after everyone helped clear the table (as it was late and they had urged Meg and the rest of the staff to go home and rest), they all said their goodbyes. Ben and Penny drove off, as did Kate and Sybil, who drove up together. Georgina had to help Grayson go to the bathroom, which is why they were left behind.

"Congrats, again," Luke said as they waited in the outer foyer of the castle. "You both will be amazing parents."

"And you?" Catherine said in a teasing voice. "Dare we ask about you and Georgina?"

The cat was out of the bag, so what was the use of hiding it? "She's mine."

Matthew grinned. "I knew it the moment she told me you came over to her place last week."

"And Sybil let it slip that she took Grayson out while you two had a romantic dinner at home," Catherine added.

"I want to take it slow," he said. "She doesn't know yet, but I'll tell her soon."

"Good idea," Matthew said, looking at Catherine. "I'm happy for you. Georgina is a wonderful person."

"This is so exciting," Catherine said. "I hope you guys become mated soon."

Luke rubbed the back of his head. "Yeah, about that—"

The sound of a vehicle approaching made them all whip their heads toward the driveway. The familiar black truck pulled up to the front, and Christina and Jason stepped out.

"I thought you said you weren't coming?" Matthew asked the pair as they approached.

"We did," Jason said, then looked at Luke. "But we figured you'd be here."

"Me?" Luke asked, confused.

"Yes." Christina's expression was grave. "We have some news. About," her gaze darted toward Matthew and Catherine, "what you asked us to look into. You probably wouldn't have liked it if we waited until morning. Should we talk in private?"

They had found something out about his pride? The thought made his chest ache. He wanted to know, but at the same time, he didn't. "Just tell me the short version."

Christina hesitated, but Jason gave her a nod. "I'm afraid we did find evidence of the Armstrong Pride in Dr. Mendle's handwritten diaries." Her voice sounded choked up. "I'm sorry. It's not good news."

Of course, it wasn't. He knew, in his gut, it wasn't going to be good. "What happened?"

"I—Georgina?" Christina frowned.

"Jason! Christina!" she greeted as she walked up to them, Grayson tagging along behind her. "I'm glad you could make it."

"What are you doing here?" she asked.

"I'll explain later," Luke said. "Now, tell me what happened."

"Grayson," Catherine interrupted, "Did I ever show you the balcony in the West wing? It's huge so the Blackstone dragons can land and take off from there."

"Oh wow! I wanna see! Can I see, Mommy?" Grayson asked.

Georgina looked confused, but she obviously sensed the gravity of the situation. "Of course."

"Let's go." Catherine took Grayson by the hand and led him away.

"Luke, what's going on?" Georgina asked.

"Are you sure you want her to hear this?" Christina asked, crossing her arms over her chest.

"It's all right," Luke said. "She can be here."

Christina shrugged. "If you say so. Anyway, it took us a while. Dr. Mendle has entries in his diaries about the Armstrong Pride from South Bend, Washington. They were written over twenty-three years ago."

He swallowed hard. "Go on."

"Dr. Mendle was there when … they captured the entire pride. Twenty in total, five of them cubs."

"What happened?"

"They were taken to a facility in California where the adults underwent some tests." Christina's voice was shaky, and her hands curled into fists. "The cubs were kept there for a year as well and then transported to Texas."

"One of the cubs escaped during transport," Jason said. "The Alpha's son. He killed half the guards and the drivers. The ones who survived chased after him, but they never found him. Colorado is halfway between California and Texas. It fits the timeline of when we found you." Jason's eyes turned to dark steely pools.

"And the rest of the pride?"

"I'm sorry, Luke," Christina said with a shake of her head. "All gone."

"Wait, I don't understand," Georgina said. "What's going on?"

"We suspect that the same people who kidnapped you and Grayson were responsible for murdering Luke's pride," Christina said.

Georgina went pale. "No ... I mean, how can you be sure?"

"We can ask Riva and Hank," Luke said in a flat tone.

"What about Mom and Dad?" Jason asked, his voice defensive.

"They knew," he spat. "They knew and didn't tell me!"

"They wouldn't do that!" Jason bit back. "They're not like that."

"They said I wasn't ready to hear it. When were they going to tell me?" The bitterness and hate were seeping into him, threatening to consume him again.

Matthew placed a hand on his shoulder. "I'm sure they had their reasons—"

Luke shrugged his shoulder. "Fuck that! They couldn't have sat me down and told me the truth? Why would they hide it from me?"

"Listen, you were the one who stayed away all these years," Jason said, his voice rising and a finger pointing at Luke's chest. "I don't know what happened or what you said that day you left, but I can still remember seeing mom sneak into the family room at night to cry! For over a year! *You* did that!"

"Stop," Matthew commanded. A chill hung in the air. His dragon was making its presence known.

Luke growled, his lion rearing up and getting ready for a fight. But he knew he wasn't a match for Jason. Besides, he'd already torn this family apart once.

His lion wasn't very happy about having to back down and

made its displeasure evident with loud growls and clawing at him from the inside. He deserved it. Deserved to have all this misery eat away at him.

"Luke."

Georgina's voice brought him back. "I have to go," he said in a hoarse whisper. "I can't ...." He felt the lion wanting to rip out of him, and he didn't want to do it here.

"Luke!"

He ignored the calls as he sped away, running into the woods behind the castle. *No*, he told the lion, *not now*. His animal would be unpredictable and out of control. He had to stay human.

Luke didn't get too far. He didn't have a plan, and he didn't know where to go. All he knew was he needed to be alone. His instinct somehow brought him to where this all began. He walked right into the thicket of trees where, as a cub, he had stumbled into the Lennox property and the four boys—Matthew, Jason, Nathan, and Ben—had found him.

Those evil bastards would pay for this, he vowed. For what they did to his pride, not to mention Georgina and Grayson, and for everything else they might have done to other shifters. He would annihilate every last one of them.

"Luke?"

He whipped around. "Georgina?"

The low branches to his left shook as they parted. Even in the dark, he recognized the figure that walked through.

Georgina sighed in relief. "They told me I might find you here."

He huffed. "You should go back. I'm sure Christina could drop you and Grayson off."

She frowned and crossed her arms over her chest. "I'm not leaving. Not until I know you're okay."

"I'm fine, all right?" he groused. "Now go." He turned away, but she circled around to face him.

"No, you're not." She placed a hand on his chest. "I'm sorry."

"You didn't do anything," he said. He thought he saw her wince. "Those people who hurt you and Grayson, they were responsible for everything."

"Then why are you out here? Why are you mad at your family—"

"They're not my family!" he roared. "If Hank and Riva cared about me, they would have told me!"

"You stubborn ass!" She pushed at his chest.

Her words caught him off guard, so he remained frozen, watching her with careful eyes.

"They did—do—care about you, don't you see?" Her eyes were rimmed with tears. "I don't know what happened and what they were thinking, but I do know what it's like to want to protect your child. What happened to your pride was awful, and there's just no good way to explain to anyone that their entire family was killed, no matter what their age. Maybe Hank and Riva were wrong and they should have told you." She paused, her breathing labored. "But parents are human and not perfect, no matter how much we want them to be. They make mistakes, too. They can only try to do the best they can in any situation."

A new emotion choked him up, one that he named easily. *Guilt.* Georgina's word struck him in the gut like a knife. And that dreaded feeling he'd been keeping inside him threatened to burst out.

He let out a roar as his hands turned into claws. He turned around and slashed at the nearest tree trunk, ripping the bark into ribbons. When he was done, he was still unsatisfied, but it felt good.

"Feeling better?"

"You're still here."

Her warm palm pressed against his back. "Of course. Where else would I be?"

He slowly turned around, as if he were afraid she'd disappear into a puff of smoke if he moved too fast. But she was here. Standing in front of him. Very real. "Georgina," he whispered.

She stepped forward, sliding her hand up his chest, until she cupped his jaw. He closed his eyes, enjoying the feeling of her warm skin. He caught her scent—that delicious smell that called to him, mixed with arousal. He let out a growl and pulled her soft body to his, bringing his lips down to hers.

Her moan of pleasure as their mouths met was like music to his ears. He wanted to make her his, right this moment, but at the same time, wanted more for her. The plan was to take her away for a weekend, somewhere beautiful and romantic where he could make love to her on a soft bed with luxurious covers for hours and hours. Not a quickie in the woods.

"Wait," he said, pulling away from her. "I wanted to do this right. For this to be perfect."

She grabbed his hands and tugged him down on the soft grass. "This *is* perfect." She leaned over and kissed him. "This is right."

He pushed her down. No, he wanted to say. She was the one who was perfect. Beautiful, kind, and perfect.

"Luke, kiss me again," she said.

He complied. How could he not? Her lips were sweeter than any dessert he'd ever tasted, and he could never get enough of her. Their mouths clashed, and when he slipped his tongue inside hers, she gasped, then moaned, pushing her body up against his so he could feel every curve.

Luke was desperate to touch her. He moved his hand between them to unbutton the front of her dress, keeping himself under control so he didn't rip it off. Without breaking their kiss, he lifted her shoulders and eased her arms out of the sleeves.

She let out a moan when he moved lower, raining kisses on her jaw and down her neck. He pulled her bra cups down to reveal her breasts, tipped with gorgeous dusky nipples which had tightened under his gaze. Her fingers dug into his hair as he took one in his mouth and teased it with his tongue. Her arousal seemed to fill the air, and the scent wrapped around him.

"Luke!" she cried out when his hand moved between her legs. He was done denying himself and her. After tugging her panties down to her thighs, he teased her soft and wet lips, making her squirm. Her fingers yanked at his scalp when he pushed a finger inside her. God, he could come just smelling her and touching her like this.

She moved her hips, obviously wanting more. His thumb found her clit, and when he stroked the engorged bud, she let out a squeal. He smothered her mouth with his lips, tasting her again as his fingers plunged into her. She tightened around him, her pussy squeezing his fingers as her orgasm razed her body. He continued to tease her and push his fingers into her, not wanting to stop until another smaller orgasm made her body shudder.

Georgina's breath slowed, and she opened her eyes. Luke lifted his fingers to his mouth, tasting her sweet juices. Her taste shot desire straight to his cock, and his erection strained painfully against his pants.

"Please, Luke, I need you."

He whipped off his shirt and made quick work of his pants and underwear, tossing them aside. His hard cock sprung free, ready to take her. He spread her knees apart and moved between her thighs. He teased her, rubbing his cock against her clit and up and down her slick lips. He had to make sure she was ready for him.

"Now, Luke," she whispered.

He covered her body with his, careful not to crush her. As he claimed her mouth again, he pushed the tip of his cock against her entrance. She was tight and hot, but slick enough to take his length. He went slow, pushing himself inside her inch by inch so she could adjust to him. Finally, he was fully inside her and he gritted his teeth to keep himself from losing control.

She sucked in a breath. "More," she pleaded, rocking her hips into him.

Luke shoved his hands into her hair, undoing her braid as he plunged his tongue into her mouth to taste her again. Slowly at first, he moved his hips, drawing out of her halfway before pushing inside again. Her body writhed underneath him, her tormented groan a heady invitation.

He moved faster, picking up his pace. She cried out, begging him for more. He slipped his hands under her sweet ass so he could lift her and drive deeper into her, letting her have what she wanted. He pulled back and slammed into her. She yelped, her body shuddering as he filled her. She was tight and slick, and his cock moving inside her brought a strangled cry from her lips. They were a perfect fit, as if they were made just for each other.

"Open your eyes."

And she did. Even in the dark, he could see her large, brown eyes were clouded with desire. He held onto her gaze, watching her as her body spasmed and exploded while he continued to thrust inside her.

Her eyes shut and her mouth opened as her orgasm came, blasting out quickly. "Luke!" Her body lifted toward his, tremors rocking her body as he kept thrusting inside her, seeking his own pleasure.

Luke let out a guttural moan that came from deep inside. It was primal and wild, and he felt his cock spasm and swell as his own orgasm made his body wrack with shudders. He exploded inside her, filling her, and she cried out again as her pussy pulsed around him. He didn't stop, couldn't stop, as he continued to thrust into her, coaxing another smaller orgasm from her.

The sensual, frenzied haze around them didn't go away, but rather, it settled over them like a warm blanket. Even as he slipped out of her, he could feel the heat between their bodies, as well as something he hadn't felt in a long time, if at all—a sense of peace and contentment.

"Georgina," he whispered. "I need to tell you something."

"Hmmm?" She smiled up at him. "What is it?"

"You're mine," he said. "My mate."

She sucked in a breath, and her eyes went wide. "I'm your mate?"

He nodded. "Do you know anything about mates?" He tried to dampen down the jealousy rearing inside him as he thought of a way to bring up what he'd been dreading to ask. "Your … Grayson's dad. He never called you that?"

She shook her head. "No. We didn't … know each other very long. We weren't in love or anything. He … passed away right after I told him I was pregnant."

"Oh." He felt some relief knowing she hadn't been anyone else's mate. However, he also felt sadness for Grayson, who never knew his biological dad. Just like he never knew his.

"I don't understand." She shook her head. "How could I be your mate? I'm not a shifter."

"You don't have to be," he said. "My lion, it recognized you as my mate the moment I laid eyes on you. At the lab."

"You knew? All this time? And you didn't say anything?"

Luke sighed and rolled onto his back. "When I first saw you with Grayson, I thought you had someone. And if Grayson had a father who was waiting for you two to come home, I wasn't going to get in between that."

"Oh."

"And after … well, I just knew I wasn't good for you. Would never be good enough for you—"

"Don't say that!" She propped herself up and then lay on his chest. "Don't say that," she repeated in a whisper, then pressed her lips over his heart.

"It's true. But," he sat up and lifted her so she straddled him, "you can be damned sure I'll do everything to make myself worthy of you."

Her face faltered. "Luke, I …."

"Yes?"

She swallowed, and he saw the pulse at her throat tick. "Nothing. I mean, we should probably head back. It's getting late. Grayson—"

He nodded. "Of course." They got up and began to gather their discarded clothes.

"It's too dark," she said, as she wiggled into her panties. "Though I'm glad you can't see my jiggly bits."

He bit his lip, trying not to remind her that he could see in the dark. Instead, he grabbed her and pressed her luscious body up against his, his hand going down to cup her ass. He wanted her again, and he let her know by brushing his semi-erect cock against her stomach. "I like all your bits."

She frowned. "Even the jiggly ones?"

"Especially those."

She laughed and pushed him away. "C'mon, let's go before they send out a search party for us."

They finished dressing, Georgina fixed her hair, and then they made their way back to the castle. Jason, Christina, and Matthew were still there, waiting by the foyer.

Matthew smirked at them. "Should I call Catherine and Grayson?"

"Yes, please," Georgina said. "We should head back; it's getting pretty late."

Matthew nodded and disappeared into the castle. Jason, who had been full of rage before, looked relaxed. He even gave Luke the same smirk. "Why the hell do I feel like Dad, back when I was a teen and he'd wait for me to come home when I snuck out?"

Christina smacked her husband on the arm, then turned to Georgina and grabbed a blade of grass sticking out from her hair. "I see you found him."

Georgina turned bright red. "Yes. I did."

Luke frowned at Christina, then put an arm around Georgina. "She knows. That she's mine."

"And you're hers," Christina reminded him. "Don't forget that."

The door opened, and Catherine walked out with Matthew, Grayson nestled in his arms. "He got excited, then fell asleep on the couch," Catherine said.

Luke grabbed Grayson from Matthew and settled the boy against him. "I'll take them home."

The drive home was silent, but comfortable. When he got to Georgina's house, he cut the engine and turned to her. "Hold on."

He got out of the driver's seat, walked over to her side, and opened the door, then helped her out. "I want to see you again."

She glanced around nervously. "Of course."

"I want us to go out. I mean, will you go out with me? I'll ask Kate or Sybil to babysit."

She nodded. "If they say yes, sure."

He slid a hand into her hair and leaned down to kiss her, savoring her taste and feel and smell, hoping to drink in enough of her to last him until they saw each other again. When he pulled away, she sighed and braced herself on his chest.

"I'll put him to bed," he said, nodding at Grayson. "You can go relax, if you want."

The young boy was dead to the world and was heavy as a rock in Luke's arms. He brought Grayson inside, all the way to his room. Laying him down on the small twin bed, Luke brushed aside a lock of reddish blond hair from the boy's face. The tendrils felt soft and delicate in his rough fingertips. A rumble came from deep within him and while the sound was unintelligible, he knew what it meant. From now on, Grayson was his, too.

"Thank you for bringing him in," Georgina said as she

entered the room. She was wrapped up in a thick, terry cloth robe.

"No problem," he said, walking up to her. "I'll see myself out. Go and get some rest." He kissed the top of her head.

"I will," she replied in a soft whisper. "Good night, Luke."

"Good night, Georgina."

CHAPTER ELEVEN

GEORGINA SAT at her desk and crossed a leg over her knee, bouncing it nervously as she watched the clock on the wall across from her. Fifteen minutes to noon.

She tried to occupy her mind, so she wouldn't notice the seconds crawling by. Of course, when she had a free moment, the only thing she could think about was Luke and last night. Making love with him was something she would never forget, something utterly indescribable. The memory would be forever burned in her mind, but she couldn't decide whether that was a good or a bad thing. On one hand, she would at least have the memory forever. But on the other hand, each time she thought of last night, she would always think of the act of betrayal she was about to commit.

Act normal. She glanced over at the window, wondering if Adrian's snipers could see her, too. Maybe she was being paranoid, but she had no doubt of just how far The Chief would go. She'd seen it with her own eyes and lived through it.

Some people might have said her past was privileged. Her

family had owned a dozen businesses on the Eastern Seaboard, and she grew up in a beautiful home with servants catering to her every whim. But looking back now, she saw what it truly was—a prison. And when she went off to college, she realized how truly sheltered she had been. Her first semester, she met Mark Mills. Georgina didn't know he was a bear shifter.

She went to a bar in the next town with her dorm mates. Mark was there with his friends, and they came over to talk to the girls. He was handsome, funny, and oh-so-smooth. Needless to say, he got into her panties real quick. The next day, they exchanged numbers. They saw each other a couple more times, mostly meeting him at his place after classes were done.

Then, a few weeks later, she started feeling sick, so she took a test. Positive. She was pregnant with Mark's baby. She told him, and that's when he confessed about being a bear shifter.

She was shocked. All her life, she'd been taught shifters were bad. They were evil abominations. The Chief had taught her that. They were not to be trusted, nor should humans mix with them. But Mark was sweet and kind; he even assured her he was going to take care of her and the baby. Georgina figured, even though she didn't love him right then, she would eventually. Not that she ever got the chance.

Pushing the memory aside, she glanced up at the clock once more. Ten minutes to noon. Matthew was at the mines for the day, but Jason was still inside his office. She had to find a way to get him out. An idea struck her. She picked up the phone and dialed his extension.

"Yes, Georgina?" Jason answered.

"Umm, Jason, Christina's office called. They said they needed you down there right away."

"Oh? Hmmm, she didn't message me or anything." There was a short pause, one that made her heart nearly stop. "All right, I'll head out then. It's almost lunchtime anyway, so I should see if she wants to get a bite."

The line went dead and a few moments later, Jason strode out of his office. "It's nearly noon," he said as he stopped by her desk. "Shouldn't you be going on your lunch break?"

"Umm …." *Get a grip.* "I just need a couple more minutes. Er, I'm waiting to call back Stevenson in the New York office."

"Oh, okay. See you later!" With a wave, Jason turned and walked out of the executive suites and into the elevator lobby.

When her heart finally stopped threatening to jump out of her rib cage, Georgina managed to calm herself. *You can do it,* she said. Oh God, she didn't want to. She forced herself to think of an image in her head. Of Mark, lying in a pool of his own blood. Then she imagined it as Grayson. And Luke.

You have to do this, she said as she stood up from her desk, her knees wobbly as a newborn foal's. She took a deep breath, looked around her (which was silly because she was all alone) and then headed into Jason's office. It was so quiet, she could only hear the soft whirring of the air conditioner. She crossed the room, the USB drive from Adrian clutched in her fist.

Kneeling down next to the CPU, Georgina opened her palm. The small piece of metal seemed heavier than it looked, and her heart was beating a thousand miles a minute as she moved her hand closer to the open port.

No!

She stood up so quickly the blood rushing to her brain made her dizzy. Bracing herself on the table stopped her from toppling over, and she bit the back of her hand to stop herself from crying out. *I can't do this.* She couldn't betray these people who had been so kind to her and Grayson, not to mention, risked their lives to save them in the first place.

Growing up, she was blind to what The Chief was really doing—that their family businesses were nothing but a front for a hate group who wanted to eradicate all shifters on earth. She found out the hard way. When she realized her parentage and where she came from, she wanted to rip out of her skin. Because how could she have possibly come from such hatred, when she carried the most precious thing in the world?

Georgina took a deep breath and smoothed her hair back. She would have to figure out another way, though really, there was only one way. Come clean. To Jason and Matthew, and to Luke. The Chief's influence was far-reaching, but surely, she and Grayson were safe in Blackstone. She hadn't done anything yet, and if she confessed now, maybe they would believe that she never had any bad intentions.

As she got ready to leave, Georgina looked around her, making sure she didn't disturb anything on Jason's desk. She scuttled toward the door, grabbed the handle and practically leapt out the door. In her haste, she didn't notice the solid figure standing by the door until she bumped into it.

"Georgina?" Luke's hands gripped her arms. "I was looking for you. I thought I heard you in there."

"You have?" Her heartbeat went wild. "What are you doing here?" He looked behind her. "Where's Jason?"

"I—"

"Georgina, we need to talk—Luke?"

Oh no. Glancing around Luke's wide frame, she saw Jason walking into the suites with Christina right behind him. Both wore serious looks on their faces.

Luke whipped around. "I'm taking Georgina and Grayson to lunch."

"You're not going anywhere," Jason said, his voice low and gravely. The temperature in the room suddenly dipped low, and Jason's silvery stare zeroed in on Georgina.

Luke took a defensive stance, placing himself in front of her. "What the fuck is going on?"

Jason ignored Luke and circled around him to face Georgina. His eyes blazed as he fixed them on her, and she could feel the immense power radiating from him. "Christina didn't call me."

She swallowed the lump in her throat and opened her mouth, but nothing came out.

"You were in my office."

"I—"

"Don't deny it!" Jason shoved his phone in front of her face. "We have live cameras in there."

Her heart dropped straight into her stomach. "I, I—" She shut her mouth when she saw herself on the small screen, walking into Jason's office and going to his computer.

"Give me that!" Luke grabbed the phone from Jason's hand.

As Luke stared at the screen, all the air rushed out of her lungs and the blood drained from her face. His expression was inscrutable, but she could see the way his jaw tightened and his eyes became as hard as steel. Slowly, he turned to her. "Tell me you have a good explanation."

What could she say? She was caught red-handed.

"What were you trying to do?" Jason asked. "And just who the hell are you?"

"I'm sorry. I wanted to tell you—"

"Don't even think of lying," Christina added, her voice icy. She tossed a brown envelope toward her, which Luke easily caught. "Someone just had that delivered. It was addressed to me."

Luke practically tore through the envelope. The photos fell onto the carpet and when she looked down, she knew this was it. The first photo was of her and Adrian in the bathroom at the park last weekend. It was compromising, to say the least. It was taken from above, like a grainy security camera, but it looked like Adrian was all over her. The next photo was much older and one she recognized. When she was just sixteen, The Chief instructed Adrian to bring her to an anti-shifter rally. She was right there, beside him, next to some people holding up signs with hateful slurs and slogans.

"That's the man who attacked us in London," Jason said, pointing to Adrian's face on the photos. "What were you doing with him? Do you know him? And The Chief? The Organization?"

The name coming from Jason's lips made her whip her head up. "You know about The Chief?"

"Dr. Mendle's diaries," Christina said. "We've had them all this time." Her icy eyes narrowed at Georgina. "Did The Organization send you here? Was it all a ruse, you being 'captured' in that lab?"

Georgina swallowed the lump in her throat. How could they even think that?

"All this time ... you were a spy? For them?" Luke roared.

"No!" She tried to grab Luke's arm, but he evaded her touch. "Please, it's not what it looks like!"

"Is Grayson even your son?" Luke asked, his hands curled into tight fists beside him.

Anger surged as his words cut into her. "How dare you! Of course, he's my son!" How could he say that? "Grayson ... he's mine. And the reason I'm here now." Tears began to flow down her cheeks and she staggered back, bracing herself against her desk. "I don't know where to begin. What to tell you."

Christina stepped forward. "Just tell us everything. It'll be easier."

Georgina wiped her eyes with the back of her hand. "I was born into it. What you call The Organization, though they don't have a name. I didn't have a choice. I'm ... The Chief is ... I'm the Chief's daughter."

Luke let out a strangled growl. "He ordered my pride killed!" He seized her arms, and she winced from the pain. "What did you know about them? Why did they kill my family?"

"I don't know!" she yelped. "I don't know anything about that, I swear!"

"Luke," Jason said, grabbing his shoulder. "Stop. You're hurting her. She was just a child when that happened."

Luke loosened his grip and let out an unhappy grunt as he stalked away from her. *Oh Luke.* She didn't understand how, but she could feel the pain radiating from him. And did it hurt. Oh God, it hurt so bad and she desperately wanted to ease his pain. But she had to make him understand.

"Luke, I swear, I didn't mean—"

"You—" Luke lunged at her but stopped himself. He let out an anguished cry. "I can't believe—" His eyes began to glow, and the muscles under his face began to shift.

"Fuck! Luke, man," Jason said. "Get out of here. We'll take care of this."

"I'm not—" An inhuman growl escaped his chest. He turned away from her, then began to stalk away.

"Luke!" she called. "Please! Don't go!"

But he didn't seem to hear her. He pushed at the doors; the

slamming sound they made as they hit the walls caused her to jump. And just like that he was gone.

Georgina covered her mouth as a tormented cry tore from her throat.

"Please, Georgina," Christina said. "Please continue and let us try to understand."

"Chris—"

Christina held a hand up to silence her mate. "Jason, I think we should listen to her."

Jason crossed his arms over his chest. "Fine. Go on."

Georgina nodded. "I didn't know, I swear. I didn't know anything until … until Grayson. My family had always spouted anti-shifter crap and growing up, I had to listen to it and believe it. Adrian—that's the man in the photos—I always thought he was just one of our bodyguards. The Chief told him to bring me to that rally, and many others like it. I was sixteen." She thought that had been the worst of it. "They tried to turn me into them and make me say hateful things. I did, but my heart wasn't into it." The Chief could tell. The Chief knew everything, of course.

"What about Grayson?" Christina asked.

"It was a college fling. Mark didn't tell me he was a bear shifter until after I told him I was pregnant. I kept it a secret from my family. I knew they were anti-shifter, but I thought, maybe once the baby came, they would change their minds." She took a deep breath and the memories began to flood back into her mind. "They found out anyway."

Oh God, the pain. It was too much. She closed her eyes and thought of Grayson. He was alive, and he was still here. "I was in class. They came in the middle of the day and yanked me out of Lit 101. The Chief was furious. They had eyes on me, knew everything. And then … they showed me a picture.

Mark. They found him and killed him." Oh God, the memories. It was too much, but she had to keep going. "They were going to take me back home and ... purify me."

"Purify?" Christina almost sounded scared.

"Get rid of the baby."

Christina's face faltered, and Jason came to her side quickly, pulling her to him. "How did you manage—"

"I escaped," she said. It was like instinct taking over, wanting to protect her baby. "They were also stupid, coming in the middle of the day." She remembered how, as they were taking Georgina away, the class period ended and suddenly all the classroom doors opened. The hallways filled with students, eager to get out of class on a Friday afternoon. With the chaos and confusion, she was able to escape from her captors.

"I ran off campus. Took whatever cash I had in my purse and bought the cheapest bus ticket I could that would take me the farthest away. I made it to Wyoming, and a nice old couple took pity on me when they found out I was pregnant and homeless. He was a veterinarian, and he hired me to be his receptionist, even though he didn't really need one." She smiled sadly, thinking about Dr. Greene and his wife Arlene. She was just glad The Chief didn't get to them. "And then ... Grayson was born. How can I even describe what that was like? Here's this person I just met, and yet I fell in love the moment I laid eyes on him. He was mine, all mine." And her world completely changed from that moment on.

"So, what were you doing in the lab?" Jason asked.

"I thought I was safe in Wyoming. And we were for five years. But then they found us again. The Chief was furious, of course, and wanted to punish me. So, I was sent to work in Dr. Mendle's lab, and he locked up Grayson in a cage. If I did anything wrong, he would threaten to hurt him." She looked at Christina and Jason, and hoped they would see the truth in her eyes. "Luke killing Dr. Mendle was the best thing that ever happened to us."

"Why didn't you tell us this from the beginning?" Jason said.

"I don't know." She shrugged. "I felt trapped. I didn't know you, any of you, and I wasn't sure I could trust you. If you found out who I was, what would you have done? You'd have locked me up, and I would have never seen Grayson again. I was planning to leave Blackstone as soon as I had the means."

Jason and Christina looked at each other but said nothing.

"I didn't know that you were good people and that you could be trusted. And then, things happened and Luke ...." It hurt, even just to say his name. "Adrian followed me. I don't know how they found me, but he said I had to do something for them." She took out the USB drive she had hidden in her pocket. "I had to put this in your computer by noon today or they would expose me."

"The pictures. They arrived when they realized you didn't do the job," Christina deduced.

"I couldn't do it," she sobbed. "I ran out of your office, and I was going to tell you everything." But she was too late. They had already seen her, kneeling by the computer, about to put the USB drive in. "I swear, I wasn't going to, but they threatened Luke and Grayson! They already killed Mark and—"

"Georgina," Christina's voice was soothing, though her eyes were rimmed with tears. She reached out and touched Georgina on the shoulder. "I believe you."

The tightness in her chest loosened, but not all the way. "Thank you." It felt good, laying it all out. Her gaze went to the doors. Oh Luke. Would he believe her, too?

"Hold on," Jason said. "So, this guy and The Organization, they're here? In Blackstone?" His eyes began to glow again, and this time, his anger wasn't directed at Georgina. "Do you know how many of them are here? Where they could be?"

"They could easily blend in," Christina pointed out. "It's high season for summer tourists."

"This doesn't sound good," Jason said. "Georgina, if you can help us—"

"Yes!" she said. "I'll do anything. Tell you anything and everything I know."

"Good," Christina said. "We can start with what you can tell us about your family."

"I will, but first you have to keep Luke and Grayson safe," she said. "Adrian said he'd hurt them if I didn't comply. He had Mark shot by a sniper as he was leaving work."

"Bastards," Jason cursed. "I'll take care of Luke, make sure he's safe."

"And Georgina and I will take Grayson to the castle," Christina said. "We'll take one of the company cars."

Jason nodded. "All right, keep me posted." He grabbed Christina and kissed her on the mouth. "I'll see you later. Stay safe."

"We will." When Jason left, Christina turned to Georgina. "Ready?"

"Let's go."

They headed to the daycare center on the second floor and quickly explained to Irene, the coordinator, that Grayson had a family emergency. After checking a confused Grayson out of the daycare, they headed to the garage.

"Thank you again," Georgina whispered to Christina. "I really appreciate this. I know you're human too, and that you don't have to get involved in this."

Christina gave her a small smile. "I'll tell you about me some other time, but for now, let's just get you two safe and sound, okay?" She led them to the service entrance in the back and pushed the door out to the garage. "We should—"

"And where do you think you're going?"

Georgina's blood turned to ice in her veins and, on instinct, she grabbed Grayson and put him behind her. Christina tensed up.

"Well, well." Adrian looked at Christina and Georgina. "You thought you could escape, did you?" He tsked. "Georgie, you were a bad girl and now you know what that means." He looked at Grayson.

"No!" she cried. "Please. Don't."

"You bastard!" Christina spat. "How dare you—"

"You are both traitors!" Adrian shouted. "And you're going to pay."

Christina lunged at Adrian, fists flying, and Georgina let out a scream. While Christina was able to land a few blows, it was no use. Adrian used his sheer size and muscle to overpower her. He flipped her around and wrapped a hand around her waist, squeezing tight. "Bitch!" He reached down to the weapon strapped at his waist.

"No!" Georgina screamed again as Adrian raised his hand and hit Christina on the head with the butt of his gun. She went limp in his arms, and he dropped her to the ground.

"Now," he said, pointing the gun square at Georgina's face, "you are going to come with me or I'll blow your pretty face off in front of your son."

"Mommy!" Grayson cried.

"Don't!" she yelled. "I'll come with you." She looked at Christina, who lay very still on the ground. "We need to help her first."

Adrian laughed. "Help her? Are you stupid? It doesn't matter. Soon, this place will be gone."

"What are you talking about? What are you going to do?"

"We've got big plans for Blackstone. We're going to get rid of every last one of these animals once and for all," he sneered, a glint in his eyes. "Now, are you going to come with me, or will I have to make you?" He shoved the gun at her face.

A cold feeling gripped her. "I said I'll come with you."

"Good girl, Georgie." He grabbed her arm. "We're going for a long ride."

CHAPTER TWELVE

Luke ran and ran, not caring where he was going as long as it was far away from *her*. Looking at her, even being around her, made him feel like his chest was caving in.

His lion roared, wanting to get out. And Luke gave in, letting the animal take over. It ripped out of him viciously, his bones cracking and skin breaking into fur, claws, and sharp teeth.

He tried to shut his mind as the lion controlled their body, but he couldn't. Georgina's betrayal burned through him like he had swallowed fire. How could she have kept it from him? That she was the daughter of that bastard.

She knew too, right before they made love. Georgina knew The Chief ordered his pride's eradication, yet she came to him. Was it all a game to her? Did she pretend to care for him and then fucked him to keep her secret? Of course, she did. The lying bitch.

It sickened him to think of Grayson. She probably got herself pregnant to manipulate another man. The Chief and his Organization really were pure evil and would stop at nothing to get what they wanted.

A loud screeching sound overhead made the lion halt in its tracks as it ran across a clearing. Power emanated from the golden creature above, making the lion freeze. *Fucking Matthew.* His lion acknowledged that Matthew Lennox was the biggest Alpha around, so no matter how much he tried to run, he couldn't.

The dragon disappeared from the sky. A few minutes later, Matthew walked out from behind the line of trees at the edge of the clearing. He was buttoning his jeans with one hand and tapping on his phone with the other.

"Change back," he commanded to the lion.

It had no choice. Luke gritted his teeth as the change came quickly, the pain shooting through his bones as he became human again. He heaved from the sudden shift, his head feeling light. He felt something hit his head—a spare set of clothes Matthew must have been carrying along with his own.

"Jason told me you ran off," Matthew said in a calm voice. "He asked all of us to try and find you. What happened?"

He grunted as he finished dressing and turned away. "Nothing."

"It's not nothing, obviously." He felt Matthew grab his shoulder. "You can tell me."

"Just leave me alone!" He shrugged Matthew's hand off. "I don't need you. I don't need anyone. I'll be fine."

"That's such horse shit!" Matthew sidestepped to face him.

There were more high-pitched screeches coming from high above. Two more dragons circled overhead, one of them identical to Matthew's dragon, while the other one was smaller, roughly half the size. They flew in unison, swooping down and disappearing. A few moments later, Jason and Sybil both walked into the clearing.

"Luke!" Sybil ran toward him and threw her arms around her. "Luke, I'm sorry. About your pride."

"There's nothing to be sorry about, Sybbie."

"I told them what happened," Jason explained. "And that you ran away before you heard Georgina's entire story."

"So you know how she betrayed us! And that she's one of *them*!" He spread his arms in challenge. "Her father was the one who killed my pride!" He turned to Matthew. "And tried to kill you, your mate, and everyone else on your wedding day!"

Jason shook his head. "Yes, she's The Chief's daughter, but she had nothing to do with any of that."

"How can you be sure?" Rage filled his veins, making his blood boil. "What if she was sent here to spy on us? And who knows what else? We caught her just in time."

"You're an idiot!" Matthew shot back. "She's your mate."

"There's no such thing as mates."

"Then why did you help me with Catherine?" Matthew countered. "And Jason with Christina? And Ben? And Nathan?"

Luke huffed, but didn't say anything.

"Look man, I know things haven't been easy for you," Jason said. "And, maybe, you helped us because you still care about us. You know we care about you, too."

"That's why we're here," Matthew said.

"Georgina told us everything. From the beginning. She didn't know how evil The Chief was or about The Organization. She was a child and a pawn. When she got pregnant with Grayson, everything changed." Jason paused. "They killed

Grayson's father and then threatened to get rid of her baby. They would have done it, if she hadn't run away."

Luke felt the muscles in his jaw tick.

"And then they threatened you and Grayson. They told her they would kill you if she didn't plant that device in my computer. She didn't do it though. I know because our systems at Lennox weren't compromised."

Shock entered his system like a slow wave. It made his temple throb and his gut clench.

"Luke, please," Sybil whispered. "Just listen to your heart. What does it say?"

Luke let out a frustrated growl. Georgina … she did it to protect him and Grayson? Of course, she did. "Dammit!" He kicked a rock with his bare foot. "She's mine." *And I love her.* He had for a long time now; he just could never say it.

"Yes!" Sybil squealed and hugged him.

"Where is she?" he asked, his throat constricting. Hopefully she would forgive him for not believing her.

"She and Grayson are headed to the castle," Jason explained. "We need to—" A ringing sound interrupted him before he could continue. He got his phone from his pocket and answered it. "Hello. Christina? What? You were *what?*" Jason's eyes started to glow, and Luke immediately felt the temperature change. He remained silent as he listened to whatever Christina was saying on the other line, even though it was obvious he was getting agitated. "Who found you … who's that? Oh, the new guy." He let out a relieved breath. "Are you okay? Yeah, he's here." He glanced at Luke. "Okay. Go to medical and get checked out. Yeah, we'll be there."

"What's wrong?" Sybil asked.

Jason slowly turned to Luke. "I'm sorry. They have her and Grayson. Knocked out Christina, too."

Rage burned through him. "Bastards."

"We'll get them back," Sybil assured him.

"We will." He had to believe it. "And then we'll make them pay." His lion roared in agreement.

The fastest way back to Lennox Corp. was flying, of course, but Luke didn't want to catch a ride with any of the dragons. He hadn't gone far, and in his lion form, he quickly crossed the miles, following Sybil, Matthew, and Jason as they flew overhead. He didn't bother to wait for the dragons to shift back before going straight to the fifteenth floor.

The Shifter Protection Agency offices were shaping up, though there were still some opened boxes littering the floor and exposed wires crossing over the carpets. The few agents there were too busy to notice him, as most of them were running around. The energy in the air was palpable, and Luke knew something was very wrong.

He strode over to the corner office, easily spotting Christina through the glass walls. She was leaning against the desk, holding an ice pack to her head as she spoke to a man Luke had never seen before.

"Luke!" She waved him inside. "Glad to see you're back." Her face was grave, and she winced as she lowered the ice pack. She nodded to the man in front of her. "This is Petros Thalassa. He's going to be my right-hand man. Petros, this is Luke Lennox."

The man pivoted on his heel to face him. Though he was a couple of inches shorter than him, Petros Thalassa showed no sign of being intimidated. He was just as wide as Luke, with his shoulders and arms straining under the formal navy suit he wore. Petros seemed to size him up, and his eyes—a strange light blue-green the color of the sea—pierced right into him. *Wolf, of course.* He felt Petros' animal growl at him, a feral snarl escaping its lips. There was something not quite right with the other man. His own lion was rearing up for a fight.

"Stop with the shifter bullshit. I grew up with it and won't tolerate it. Now," Christina said. "We've got more important things to work on."

Petros gave her a nod. "Of course, Miss Stav—I mean, Christina."

Luke took a step forward. "What happened? Where are they?"

She let out a sigh. "I'm sorry. I tried to stop him." She sank down on the leather chair behind the desk. "He got away and took Grayson and Georgina."

"Christina!" Jason burst in through the office and ran toward his mate. "Are you okay? Did he hurt you? I swear I'm going to tear him—"

"I'm fine," she said, sighing as Jason pulled her into his arms. "I got checked out at the clinic."

"What happened?" Matthew asked as he and Sybil entered the room.

Christina recounted how Adrian had been waiting for them and knocked her out cold. "And then when I woke up, Petros was standing over me."

"I had just arrived," the wolf shifter explained. "And I saw a delivery truck speeding away from the garage. I felt something was off, so I followed where it had come from. Christina was on the ground. I immediately took her into the building."

Jason gave the man a grateful nod. "Thank you."

"What else did you see?" Luke asked. "Did you see a

woman and a child?"

Petros shook his head. "I'm afraid not. And I didn't think to follow the truck or read its license plate. My apologies."

"You didn't know," Matthew said. "Now, we need to figure out where they're taking Georgina and Grayson."

"Our team has started the search," Christina said. "We're tapping into every security camera in the city to see if we can find the truck matching the description Petros provided."

"Any luck?" Sybil asked.

"We're working on it, but if they took the old highways, we won't be able to track them."

"Which they probably did," Luke said. These bastards were too smart.

"We'll keep trying," Christina said. "But there's something else."

"What is it?" Luke asked.

"Even though he knocked me out, I was still semi-conscious. I heard him say something." She took a deep breath. "I think they're planning something. Something big."

"Like an attack?" Matthew asked.

"I didn't hear much, but it sounded bad. Blackstone could be in danger."

"We can't underestimate them," Jason said. "We'll have to get organized. Get everyone on board."

"We should call Dad," Sybil said. "And everyone else. Uncle James, Uncle Clark, Nathan, and Violet."

Matthew nodded in agreement. "We'll need everyone we can trust."

Luke clenched his fists. "We'll stop them." They had to. He would rescue Georgina and Grayson, kill The Chief, and then destroy every single person in the Organization. Only then would everyone he loved be safe.

CHAPTER THIRTEEN

THEY HAD BEEN DRIVING for what seemed like hours. Adrian had thrown them into the back of a dirty truck and shut the door. Since there were no windows, she couldn't see outside.

Grayson wouldn't stop crying and shaking. "I don't ... want to ... go back in the cage, Mommy."

"Shhh ... it's going to be okay, sweetie," she soothed, running a hand down his back. "I won't let them hurt you again." She didn't know how or what she would do, but she knew she would use her last dying breath to protect him if she had to.

Part of her was clinging to the hope that, maybe, someone would rescue them. Maybe it might even be Luke. But she couldn't count on that. If Adrian had taken Christina, Jason would have burned the world to get his mate back. He was smart, not provoking the dragon.

Grayson eventually tired himself out from crying and fell asleep. She held him tighter and kissed the top of his head. She had to think of a way for him to escape. Maybe once they stopped and the doors opened, she could get him to shift and run away.

Before she could even formulate a plan, the truck jerked and stopped. *Oh no.* There was no time now. Should she wake him and tell him to go?

The metal doors screeched as they opened. Georgina shielded her eyes as light filled the truck, blinding her temporarily. Even though she couldn't see, there was no mistaking the sound of guns cocking. She put her hand down, and her blood pressure plunged when she saw the half dozen gun barrels pointed at them.

"Get up," Adrian said. "We're here."

She picked up Grayson, who had begun to stir. "Mommy?" He opened his eyes and when he looked around, his face turned into pure terror.

"Shhhh, sweetie. It's okay." She held onto him tighter as she hopped off the back of the truck. Looking around, she saw they were somewhere rural. Definitely not the city.

Adrian grabbed her by the elbow and dragged her along. "Looks like we got here in time for a little family reunion."

Dread filled Georgina. She knew what he meant.

After a few minutes of walking down a dirt road, they came across an old farmhouse. He led her up the rickety porch steps, and the lone guard standing outside opened the door as they walked in. It was abandoned, judging from the dank and musty smell, though it looked like someone had straightened up and cleaned the place recently.

Adrian pushed her along and shoved her into one of the rooms. When he tried to grab Grayson, she screamed and clawed at him, but it was no use. Adrian wrenched Grayson away from her.

"The Chief wants to talk to you in private," he said as he walked away.

"No! Grayson!" She turned around to go after them.

"Hello, Georgina."

The sound of the voice made her freeze. A chill ran over her skin.

The Chief stood up from behind a large wingback chair and turned to face her. "What? Nothing to say to your mother, after all these years?"

"What would I ever say to you?" Georgina spat.

Regina Winnick's red-painted lips curled into a smile, though her eyes remained cruel and cold. "So, that was him? The cub?" she sneered. "Your abomination of a child should—"

"Shut up, Regina!"

"My, aren't you feisty now?" She walked closer to her. "Too bad you didn't show this much spirit when you were a child." She tried to place a hand on Georgina's shoulder, but she shrugged it away. "If you had only shown some backbone, you could be the one taking over once I'm gone."

"Shown some backbone? You mean spew hate at innocent people, right?"

"They're not innocent, and they're *not* people!" Regina countered. "You were always a spineless, sniveling weakling. I told your father when he was alive that he always spoiled you too much. I was always ashamed to call you my daughter! You could never have been the next Chief!"

"So, what was the plan, then?" Georgina asked. "Marry me off to your loyal right hand man and make me into some broodmare? To further our abhorrent family line?"

"You insolent child!" Regina's eyes became narrow slits. "How dare you speak that way about our family. We've been protecting the interests of human kind for generations! My father and his father before him have done everything they could to keep our bloodline pure. You were the one that muddied it with this monstrosity."

"Fuck you, Regina! Fuck you and your pure bloodline!" That earned her a resounding slap.

"You ungrateful girl!"

Georgina covered her face with her palm, trying to soothe the pain. "Why couldn't you leave us alone, Regina? I was staying out of your way, trying to raise my son. What do you want with me?"

"You stupid child!" she raged. "After what you did, becoming pregnant by one of those animals, how do you think that made me look? To our allies and the people under me? You made me into a fool!" She grabbed her arm, digging her fingers painfully into Georgina's arm. "I looked weak, especially when you escaped."

"Do what you want with me, but please, don't hurt my son," Georgina pleaded.

"Oh, I'm going to do what I want all right," Regina said with a curl of her lip. "And soon, I won't look weak to anyone. Not after I destroy Blackstone and burn it to the ground."

"No!" she shouted. "What are you planning?"

"Those stupid shifters!" Regina cackled. "They thought they were safe in their little town. We've been working for weeks, infiltrating them. That USB you were supposed to put in Jason Lennox's computer would have granted us access to the Shifter Protection Agency's network. But it doesn't matter because they will all be gone soon. We've planted powerful bombs around town. They'll never find all of them in time. In twenty-four hours, Blackstone will be no more."

"You bitch!" Georgina screamed. "You can't do that!"

"I already have, my dear daughter," Regina said. "When we detonate those bombs, Blackstone will be wiped off the earth."

"What makes you think you'll get away with this?" Georgina asked. "You can't eradicate an entire town and think people will look the other way."

"Georgina, you really have no idea what we're capable of, do you? We've spent decades buying influence and amassing power. Half the major news organizations are in our pockets, not to mention law enforcement and politicians. We've already prepared all the news reports, detailing the terrible accidents in the blackstone mines that destroyed the entire town and everyone in it."

"No one will believe you!"

"Do you think this is the first time we've done this? I've made entire groups of shifters disappear, just like that!" Regina snapped her fingers. "That lion you've been fucking? Who do you think ordered his pride to be annihilated? I didn't realize he was the cub who escaped, but when Hank and Riva Lennox started poking around, I put two and two together. They were relentless, trying to find more information. I threw them a big enough bone so they would go away."

Georgina gritted her teeth. Regina really was evil and hateful.

She continued. "We've never done something on this scale, of course, but then, there's no other town like Blackstone. Even if it came out that Blackstone was attacked on purpose, no one will ever trace it to us. We already have scapegoats from those anti-shifter groups ready to take the fall. I'll be the first Chief to finally rid the world of these monsters."

"You're the monster!" Georgina screamed.

Regina rolled her eyes. "This is getting tiresome. Adrian!"

"Yes, Chief?" Adrian said as he strode into the room.

"Take her away," Regina ordered. "Make sure she and the brat stay put."

"Will do." Adrian trained his dead eyes at her. "Let's go."

"Don't touch me!" She evaded his grasp.

Adrian ignored her and took her by the arm. He led her out of the room and up to the second floor of the farm house. They walked down a long hallway, and Adrian pulled a rope hanging from above. A ladder slid down from the ceiling.

"Mommy!" Grayson cried as he peeked from the attic above.

"Grayson! Did they hurt you?" She yelped as Adrian pushed her forward.

"Get up there," he ordered.

At least I'll be with Grayson. She grabbed the ladder and made her way up. She gathered Grayson into her arms and hugged him tight.

"Don't even think of trying to escape," Adrian warned as he stared up at them. "We've got guards everywhere."

Georgina startled when the ladder closed shut with a loud bang.

"Mommy, where are we?" Grayson asked, tears streaming down his cheeks. "I don't want to be here. I wanna go back to Blackstone, to our house. And to Luke and Auntie Sybil and—"

"I'm sorry, sweetie," she said, kissing his temple. "I'm so sorry."

"Did the bad men get us again?"

She nodded. "I'm afraid so. But I'm not going to let them hurt you or put you in a cage again."

"How, Mommy?"

Good question.

"Is Luke gonna come rescue us? Or Auntie Kate and Sybil?"

"I don't know, sweetie. They might not … know we're in trouble." The lie sounded better than the truth, which was they might not even care about them. Luke had been hurt by her supposed betrayal. Surely, they would side with him?

The look on Grayson's face made her heart clench. "I think they will," he said in a small but confident voice.

Oh God, they might not even live long enough to rescue them. What Regina was planning—

She curled her fingers into fists. No, she couldn't let her win. She couldn't let Luke and everyone in Blackstone die. But what could she do?

"Mommy?"

Grayson! A plan formed in her head. It could be risky, but it would give him a chance to live, too. It would give everyone a fighting chance.

"Wait here," Georgina said, placing him on the floor. She walked over to the only window in the attic. It was dirty and rusty, but the glass slid open. Hope surged in her. "Grayson!" she called. There was no time to lose.

Grayson got up and scampered toward her. "Mommy? Are we going to excape through the window?"

She knelt down and caressed his face. "Mommy's too big, Grayson, but you'll fit."

It took a second, but the little boy realized what she was trying to say. "No, Mommy! I won't leave you!"

"Shhh!" She hugged him close. "You have to escape, sweetie; it's the only way."

"But—"

Another idea struck her. She hoped it would work. "I have

an important mission for you. Everyone in Blackstone is in danger."

His eyes went wide. "The bad men?"

She nodded. "Yeah, the bad men want to hurt the people in Blackstone, but you can help save them."

"How?"

"When you go out that window, you shift into your bear, okay?" She knew he would be protected in that form. "And then you run. There are guards everywhere, but they might think you're just a lost cub."

"Where should I go? To the police?"

"No!" Damn, that was the kink in her plan. Regina could have the local police in the area in her pockets. That was their modus. It was how they were able to track down Mark. "Wait." There was one place they wouldn't have thought to infiltrate. "If you find a town, go to their Fire Department. You remember what that looks like in Blackstone, right?"

He thought for a moment. "That's the big brick building we drive by, right? With the red trucks and the men in hats?"

"Smart boy," she said proudly. "Ask them to call Chief Will Mason of the Blackstone Fire Department. Tell them you'll only speak to him." Hopefully that would be enough.

"Mommy, I don't know if I can do it."

"You can, sweetie. I believe in you." She hugged him tight. "You're smart and strong. Just like Luke said, right?"

He nodded. "I'll try."

"When you talk to Will, tell him everyone in Blackstone is in danger." She lowered her voice. "Tell them there are bombs planted everywhere. Can you do that?"

"Yes, Mommy."

"Good. We'll wait until the sun sets before you escape."

Georgina closed the window and walked back to the other

side of the room. At one point, some surly-looking guard came up to bring them food. Georgina gave all hers to Grayson, knowing he was probably starving and would need the energy. They waited until it was dark outside before they walked back to the window.

Georgina made him recite everything twice. When she was satisfied, she lifted him up to the window. "Crawl down to the roof, then—see that pipe?—use it to shimmy down." She buried her nose in his hair and breathed deep, trying to memorize his scent. "I love you, Grayson."

"I love you, Mommy."

She swallowed the tears in her throat as she helped him out of the window. It was hard to see through the small opening and the dirty glass, but she watched him shimmy down, crawl across the roof, and disappear off the edge.

A few seconds later, a small brown, furry blur scampered across the field. Her heart leapt into her throat and she gripped the window tight. When Grayson's bear dashed into the trees, Georgina allowed herself to breathe.

Run, Grayson. Run as fast as you can.

Sheer exhaustion made Georgina fall asleep. She stayed up all night, pacing the attic, until finally, she curled up in a corner and closed her eyes. She didn't wake up until she felt a kick to her side.

"You stupid slut!" Regina raged.

Georgina clutched at her middle, the pain blooming over her side. She looked up. Faint light was filtering into the attic from the window. It was morning. Hopefully Grayson had made it.

Regina's fingers dug into Georgina's arms like talons and hauled her to her feet. "Where is the boy?"

"Somewhere you'll never find him!" she screamed back.

"Why you—" Regina let out a frustrated sound. "It doesn't matter anyway. One boy is of no consequence, especially when we're about to make thousands more like him disappear." She gave a cruel laugh. "And guess what, dear daughter? I have front row tickets for you to the show. You're going to watch Blackstone turn to nothing but a crumbling pile of ash." She nodded to Adrian. "Take her to the car."

She felt the blood drain from her face. Oh God. Regina really was an evil bitch.

CHAPTER FOURTEEN

"I'D TELL you to go home and get some rest," Matthew said as he sat down next to Luke, "but I know that—a—you don't really sleep and—b—you'd never listen to me."

"Would you, if it were Catherine?" Luke asked.

"I wouldn't." Matthew put a hand on his shoulder. "I didn't."

Luke didn't fail to see the irony of the two of them switching positions. It wasn't too long ago that Matthew refused to rest when Catherine was in danger. Luke had known Matthew would never leave her side, so he kept him company at the hospital as they waited.

"We'll find them." Matthew gave him a squeeze.

"I know." *We have to*, he added to himself.

They worked all night, trying to find any trace of the truck that had taken Georgina and Grayson away. The Organization had somehow stolen the truck from one of their regular cafeteria suppliers and snuck into the building. They were able to follow the vehicle as it left Lennox and drove down the road, but, as they suspected, the truck turned onto the old highway that didn't have any surveillance cameras. They expanded their search but knew the trail was getting cold with each moment they were gone.

Twenty-three hours, thirty-six minutes, forty-five seconds. That was how long Georgina and Grayson had been gone. His lion let out an angry roar. It wanted them back. *I want them back too.* And when he got his hands on The Chief, he was going to rip him in two.

"Any news?" Matthew asked Jason as he came up to them. They had all camped out in Christina's office.

Jason shook his head. "No, sorry. Except that Mom and Dad and everyone are almost here. They'll be touching down in thirty minutes. Ari Stavros' jet just landed at the airstrip. They were able to pick up Nathan and Violet in Eritana."

"Do we have any ideas or clues as to what The Organization is planning? What do Mendle's diaries say?"

Jason shook his head. "Nothing yet." Jason glanced at Luke. "But don't worry, we're all working on it."

"I know." Everyone had been working hard. He knew that even Blackstone P.D. was working overtime to try and find clues as to where Georgina or Grayson could have gone. A couple of people had spotted the truck outside town, but that was the last they heard.

"Luke!" Christina rushed into the office with Sybil right behind her. "You have a call."

"Me?"

"They tried you at the mines. Ben routed the call to me." She shoved her phone at him.

"Who is it?"

"A Chief Will Mason."

Mason? Why would he call me? He took the phone from Christina. "Hello."

"Luke Lennox?" came the voice on the other line.

"Yeah."

"My name is Will Mason. I'm the Chief of the Blackstone Fire Department."

"I know who you are. What do you want?"

"I got a call from the chief over at Meadow Falls. They're about two hundred miles south of us. They said a young cub came into their station and asked them to call me."

Luke shot to his feet. "Grayson!"

"Is this the cub P.D.'s been looking for?" Mason asked.

"Was there a woman with him? You know her. Georgina."

Mason paused. "Mills? Georgina Mills? Kate's friend?"

"Yeah, that's her."

"Let me ask. Hold on." There was a pause. "Yeah. Grayson Mills. But no, he arrived alone."

Luke realized that Grayson either escaped somehow or Georgina helped him. His mate was smart too, making him go to the Fire Department instead of the police. "The boy's safe?"

"He's fine, they said. Do you want us to pick him up?"

It would probably take hours to drive there and they didn't have that kind of time. "We'll get him. If you could tell Meadow Falls to expect us, that would be great."

"Roger that. I'll let them know. And if you need anything, just call."

When the line went dead, he handed the phone back to Christina. "They found Grayson." He quickly explained what happened.

"We need to go get him now," Sybil said. "I'll go. It shouldn't take me too long."

"I'll go with you," Luke said. "If you don't mind having a passenger."

Sybil smiled warmly at him. "Not at all. Let's go get him!"

It didn't take more than fifteen minutes of flying to get to Meadow Springs. The dragon gently laid Luke down in front of the Meadow Falls F.D. Headquarters. It disappeared behind the firehouse, and a minute later, Sybil emerged, buttoning up her blouse.

They didn't waste any more time before heading into the firehouse. Luke immediately spotted Grayson, wrapped up in a blanket on one of the bunks in the corner.

"Luke!" he cried as he threw the blanket off and jumped into his arms.

Luke caught him and held him close, breathing in his familiar scent. "I'm glad you're safe."

"They have Mommy," he cried, tears pouring down his cheeks. "She made me excape. I wanted to be smart and strong."

"You were," he said, pressing his lips to his hair. "Where is she?"

"They still have her," he whispered. "The bad men."

"We need to find her. Do you remember where she is?"

"I can't," he cried. "I'm sorry. Mommy said to just run and find the nearest fire station."

"It's all right," he soothed. "We can figure it out." He looked over at Sybil, who was talking to an older man, most likely the fire chief. She gave Luke a nod, indicating she was taking care of things. With her background as a social worker, she was probably used to these kind of situations, which is why he was glad she was here.

"Mommy told me to tell you something else," Grayson said. "She said there were bombs. Everywhere in Blackstone."

Fear, real and palpable, coursed through him, followed by a shot of adrenaline. "Sybil!" he called, dashing toward her. "We need to go. Now."

Sybil looked surprised but nodded. "Thanks for your help, Chief Watson," she said.

Luke was already on his way out, Grayson in his arms. "Have you flown before?"

Grayson's eyes became as wide as saucers. "No! Are we flying?"

Luke nodded. "We're catching a ride with Auntie Sybil." He nodded toward the figure who darted behind the firehouse building. Seconds later, a large golden dragon emerged.

"Hold on to me," he said to Grayson. "Close your eyes if you get scared."

Small arms wrapped around his neck as Luke ran toward the middle of the parking lot. Sybil's dragon landed on the asphalt, and though only half the size of a male dragon, it was still quite large.

"Ready," he said with a nod.

The dragon flapped its wings and hovered a few feet off the ground. A scaly hand wrapped around Luke and Grayson. With a loud *whoosh*, they lifted off into the sky.

It was a good thing they were both shifters and their bodies easily adjusted to the cold air. Sybil flew relatively low, perhaps to not shock Grayson too much with the height. Fifteen minutes later, they arrived outside Lennox Corp. headquarters. Sybil set them down gently on the ground.

"You okay, buddy?" Luke asked Grayson as he set the boy

down. He handed the clothes back to the dragon, wrapping them around one claw.

"That. Was. Awesome!" Grayson cried. "Can we go flying again? Please Auntie Sybil?"

The dragon tossed its head and let out a cry.

"I think that means yes," Luke said, unable to stop the smile from spreading on his face. The dragon snorted, steam coming out of its nose, and then lifted off the ground to fly away. "But not right now."

"Luke!" He turned his head. Christina was running toward them. "Is he safe? Where's Georgina?" She let out a cry of relief when her eyes landed on Grayson.

Luke picked up Grayson again. "We need to talk."

"Everyone's here," she said. "Let's go."

They went inside and headed straight to the fifteenth floor. When Christina said everyone was here, she wasn't kidding. Hank, Riva, Clark Caldwell, James Walker, Ben, Nathan, Violet, Ari Stavros and his three sons, Petros, and of course, Matthew and Jason, were crammed into the office.

Riva's gaze flickered at Grayson, then she looked at Luke. He sighed. He didn't have time for this now. He set the boy down. "We're all in danger," he said. "Georgina sent a message through Grayson. The Organization has planted bombs all over Blackstone. Enough to level the entire town, I'm guessing."

"How could that be?" Hank said. "How could no one notice?"

"We weren't expecting it," Ari Stavros said. "They've probably been doing it for weeks."

"What should we do?" Clark asked.

"The bombs probably aren't like the one at the wedding,"

Nikos, the youngest Stavros, offered. "If they wanted something they could easily hide but would cause a lot of damage, then they would plant smaller bombs. The last time they tried to do it, the timer tipped us off, so the explosives would most likely have to be remotely detonated, one by one in waves so as not to disrupt the radio signals. They would also have to be in the area. Anywhere from a hundred to a thousand yards from each bomb."

"We need to start searching," Petros said. "We take a map of Blackstone, divide it into grids and break up into teams."

"We don't have enough manpower to search everywhere," Hank pointed out.

"We ask for volunteers," Petros suggested. "From the able-bodied citizens of your town. But we should also evacuate the children, the old, and the sick."

"Definitely," Hank agreed.

"This could work," Jason said. "Plus, with me, Matthew, Dad, and Sybil overhead, we can widen the search."

Time was running out, but Luke had to admit this was the best way to go about this. They had to save Blackstone. And then, he was going to find Georgina.

"Nikos, Hank, Matthew," Petros began. "You three should find a map and figure out if there are any areas which may be better to hide a bomb and could do the most damage. Bridges, dams, transportation depots, high rises and—"

"Sorry we're late!" Kate breezed in with Sybil right behind her. "Motherfuckin' client wouldn't let me off the phone. Kept droning on and on about how he hated the GUI I made. I told him to stick it up his ass and—" She stopped in her tracks, her mouth hanging open.

Luke frowned and followed Kate's gaze, which was fixed on Petros. The wolf shifter tensed and a muscle in his jaw ticked. Kate, on the other hand, went red and quickly shut her mouth.

"Petros?" Christina said. "You were saying?"

The wolf shifter shook his head. "Yes. I mean," he cleared his throat, "while they do that, we should break up into teams of two. We should lead teams of volunteers to scout the grids."

Christina nodded in agreement. "Let's get started."

CHAPTER FIFTEEN

GEORGINA SAT IN THE CAR, shifting her weight to relieve her discomfort. They had been driving for hours, first through small back roads, then country highways. When they hopped on the expressway, she started recognizing the signs and figured out where they were—somewhere south of Blackstone. If she had to guess their current location, she'd say they were just on the outskirts of town.

"Many of our people would give their right arm to be here," Regina said. "To witness the destruction of this Godforsaken town."

Georgina remained quiet, refusing to engage her mother. No, she had to save her strength. The cogs in her brain were moving a mile a minute, trying to find a way to escape or to stop them.

The car drove up the mountain pass, going higher and higher, and veering off onto a small back road. A few minutes later, they emerged onto a lookout with a clear view of Blackstone below.

Regina dragged her out of the car and shoved her toward the edge. "Go ahead and watch, dear daughter."

Oh God, this was it. She was going to watch Blackstone's destruction as it happened.

Adrian stood beside them and took out his phone. "Detonators ready? First wave on standby. All right, on my signal. Three. Two. One."

Georgina braced herself, waiting for the sounds of loud explosions, but they didn't come.

"Team Epsilon! Gamma! Delta!" Adrian shouted into the phone. "What the fuck is going on?"

"What's wrong?" Regina screeched. "Why aren't the bombs going off?" She grabbed the phone from Adrian's hands and tapped on the screen. "You morons! What's going on? Who is this?"

"This is Bleecker, Epsilon team leader. S-s-sorry, Chief!" came the crackly voice though the speaker. "It's … they must have found the bombs and disabled them somehow."

"No!" Regina howled. "All of them? How could this have happened?"

"Someone must have tipped them off," Adrian said.

Regina turned her hateful gaze toward Georgina. "You stupid bitch! You did this! Did you send your spawn out to warn them?"

"I told you you weren't going to get away with this." Shock and elation were coursing through Georgina, though she knew she wasn't out of the woods yet.

Regina let out an indignant shriek. "You ungrateful—"

"Sir!" Bleecker's voice on the phone cut through the air. "Sir! Only the bombs' remote detonation have been deactivated. They can still be set off manually. All of them have a ten second default timer."

Regina's mouth curled up into a cruel smile. "Looks like it's not over yet. Send what men we have and secure the bombs," she barked into the phone. "Don't detonate them. Wait for further instructions."

"Chief, what are you planning?" Adrian asked.

"We will have our men set off the bombs, but first, we're going to pay those animals a visit. So they know exactly who's going to wipe their existence off the face of the planet."

"Ten seconds isn't enough time!" Adrian protested.

"I know that!" She grabbed Georgina. "We will take hostages, to make sure they don't follow us. I'm sure one of our labs could use more test subjects. I bet a female dragon would highly interest our scientists."

"You monster!" Georgina cried.

"You shut your mouth!" Regina smacked her across the cheek. "Get in the car. Maybe if I'm feeling generous, we won't leave your spawn behind."

As they drove down to Blackstone, Regina continued to give orders to her men in Blackstone. "Secure as many hostages as you can find. I don't care how many, just round up whoever you can."

"Yes, ma'am. We found a couple of people trying to evacuate. We have them in custody now."

"Good. Now, what about the bombs?"

Bleecker paused. "We've secured about half of them, ma'am."

"They weren't guarded?"

"No ma'am. Looks like the receivers were destroyed, but the bombs were not disabled."

"Good," Regina said. "Have your men on standby and get ready for my signal."

There was a pause. "Ma'am, they're only set for ten seconds."

"I know that, idiot," Regina said. "Do it."

"Y-y-yes, ma'am."

"Now round up whoever's free and tell them to go down to Main Street."

"Chief, I'm sorry but this is going too far," Adrian said from the driver's seat. "What's the point of this? We should leave now and cut our losses—"

"No, we will not!" Regina said. "I'm going to make a point to these creatures. A lesson they need to learn."

"But if they're dead—"

"Silence! Am I not The Chief?"

Adrian's jaw hardened, and his mouth set into a grim line. "Yes."

"Then do as I say."

"Yes, ma'am." Adrian kept his eyes on the road and remained silent.

As they drove down Main Street, Georgina couldn't help the creepy vibe that came over her. The streets were completely empty—no one walking down the sidewalks, no cars parked, and most of the shops' doors shut and the window shades down. At the far end of the street, however, two dozen men in combat gear holding high-powered rifles were already waiting, lined up in two rows.

"Stop!" Regina said, then the car halted. "Give me your gun."

Adrian hesitated, but handed his pistol to her. Regina cocked it and pointed it at Georgina. "Move."

Georgina got out of the car, shaking as she felt the butt of the gun pressed into the back of her head. "What are you planning?"

"Did I tell you to speak? No!" She stabbed at her, the metal digging into her skull.

Regina pushed her out into the middle of the empty street, between the row of soldiers. Adrian followed behind her. "Come out, you filthy animals!" She screamed. "Come out, or I'll kill your dirty whore!"

Georgina looked at Regina. Her face was red, and her eyes were unfocused. *Oh God.* Clearly, her mother had gone insane. That also meant she was unstable and unpredictable.

"Let her go!"

Georgina's heart soared at the sound of the voice. *Luke.*

He was walking down Main Street toward them, wearing only his jeans. His hair was wild, flowing down his shoulders, and he wore a focused expression on his face. He didn't even pay attention to the rifles pointing straight at him.

"Ah, look who it is," Regina said. "Your shifter lover."

"Who are you?" he asked, his head cocking to the side.

Regina laughed. "Your worst nightmare. I'm The Chief."

Luke seemed taken aback.

"Why are you looking at me like that? Is it because you think The Chief can't be a woman?" She tsked.

"Why are you doing this? She's your daughter!" Luke roared. "And Grayson is your grandson!"

"Shut your mouth!" Regina waved the gun wildly. "That creature is not my grandson! He may have my blood flowing through his veins, but he's not one of us!"

"What do you want?" Luke asked.

"Why, I want you all to die," Regina stated matter-of-factly.

"We've disabled all your bombs, lady," Luke pointed out.

"You've disabled the remote devices," she countered. "As we speak, my men have secured the bombs and will detonate them manually. As soon as we're out of here, of course."

"Then why come here?" Luke asked.

"So that the last person you see before you die is me," she said. "Don't even think of trying to stop me. My men have hostages, the people trying to evacuate before the bombs went off. All I have to do is give the signal and they will start killing every single one of them. We can start with her." She shoved Georgina toward Adrian and then pointed the gun at her.

As Georgina toppled against Adrian, she felt something hard press against her hip. A knife! Adrian always kept one strapped around his left thigh. Without a thought, she grabbed the handle, slipped it out of the holder, and into the sleeve of her blouse as Adrian steadied her. Nerves were making her hands shake, and she prayed Adrian was too distracted to notice.

"No!" Luke roared. "If you hurt her, I'll kill you!"

"Want to try me, shifter?" Regina taunted as she cocked the gun.

Luke stared her down but didn't say a word.

"I didn't think so."

As a pause hung in the air, Georgina knew this was her chance. "Luke!" she called as she took the knife and swung it behind her, plunging it into Adrian's shoulder. She ducked and rolled away as he yelped with pain. Georgina landed face down on the pavement.

"No!" Regina screeched, then turned to the armed men. "Fire! Kill him!"

Georgina's screams were drowned out by the sound of gunfire. *Luke! No!* She hoped he would run away, but she doubted it. Luke would never run.

The gunfire seemed to go on and on. *Why would they need so much firepower to kill one shifter?* She got her answer when she looked up.

In the middle of the street was a gigantic dragon. It must have been fifty feet high, with golden, armor-like scales all over its body and a spiky tail and head. The men were continuously shooting at the dragon, but it was no use. The bullets just bounced off its plated scales.

Finally, when they ran out of bullets and the shooting stopped, the dragon opened its mouth and inhaled a breath. Fire and lava rained down from its massive maw, destroying everything in its path.

Regina let out an indignant shriek. "Get up!" she said to Adrian, who was on his knees, clutching his shoulder.

"It's all over, Chief," Adrian said. "I've tangled with a Blackstone dragon once and lived. I don't think I'll get a second chance."

"You idiot!" She turned to Georgina. "This is all your fault! You—"

A loud roar made Regina freeze and turn. A figure leapt out from the dragon flames.

Luke.

The lion pounced on Regina, sending her to the ground. As her screams filled the air, Georgina covered her ears and closed her eyes, but she was unable to stop the tears from pouring down her cheeks. Then the screams ceased.

Georgina's eyes flew open, though she kept her cheek pressed to the ground. A shadow loomed over her.

"Georgina."

She looked up. "Luke."

Strong arms wrapped around her and picked her up, setting her on her feet. She looked up at him, searching his face.

"The Chief—"

"Is still alive."

She blinked. "Huh?" Glancing around him, she saw several men in blue police uniforms taking her mother and Adrian away.

"I couldn't kill her. She's still your mother," Luke said with a shake of his head.

"Oh Luke!" She pressed her face against his chest, feeling the warmth of his skin. "I wanted to tell you. I was going to confess everything and—"

"Shh," he soothed, running a hand down her back. "It's over. It's all over. You're safe, and that's all that matters."

"Grayson found a way to get to you, didn't he?"

He nodded. "He's safe."

"Thank God." She knew in her heart he would make it.

"Georgina, I never thought I'd see you again. I'm sorry. For what I said. For not believing you."

"I'm just glad everything's okay. And that it's over." She shivered, thinking of the events of the last twenty-four hours.

Luke pulled her close. "You're safe now. I'm not going to let anything happen to you and Grayson. Georgina, I love you. And I want you to be mine. And Grayson, too."

She sucked in a breath. It took a few seconds for his words to register. "I love you, too," she blurted out. "Oh. I—"

He captured her mouth before she could say anything else. As his lips settled on hers, a zing went up her spine. She couldn't describe it, other than it set her body alight, like a lightning bolt setting the sky ablaze for a brief second. After that, however, as Luke's arms wound around her, warmth spread through her. Slow at first but building and covering her from head to toe.

When Luke pulled away, his face was that of complete shock. "Georgina ... I think it happened."

"Huh?" She was still dizzy from his kiss.

"We're mates. What we felt, it's called the mating bond." Luke took her hand and put it over his chest. She could feel his heart, like it was beating right in her hand. It startled her at first, but then she realized how amazing it felt. How it was like she could *feel* Luke, with every fiber of her being.

"Luke, I've never felt like this before."

"Me neither." He leaned down to press his lips to her, less urgent this time, but nonetheless intense.

Georgina would have been happy to keep kissing Luke, but she could tell there were more people arriving at the scene. There was so much they needed to do now, though for the life of her, she couldn't think of what right at this moment. Even as she tried to pull away, Luke only held her tighter. However, an indignant screech made her pull away and blink. She cocked her head to the side.

"Put me down, you—you—*caveman!*" Kate shrieked. Or at least, Georgina thought it was Kate. The young woman hanging upside down from the very large (and very serious-looking) man's shoulders had dark blonde hair with pink tips and sounded very much like the wolf shifter. "What the hell do you think you're doing?" Kate pounded her fists on his broad back.

The man was silent and didn't even flinch. He ignored her protests and continued to stride with purpose behind the Main Street Gift Shop, disappearing from view as Kate's wails became fainter.

"What the fuck?" Nathan Caldwell growled. He had arrived just in time to see his sister being carried away. "That asshole is kidnapping my sister! Someone get—"

"Nathan, love," Violet interrupted, placing a soothing hand

on his arm, while her other arm clasped around his waist. "It's all right."

"What do you mean it's all right?" Nathan tried to pry her hand away, but her grip was tight.

Violet laughed. "He's her mate. Didn't you notice when she walked in the office?"

Nathan's mouth hung open. "What. The. Everliving. *Fuck.*"

Georgina felt a rumble, and when she looked up at Luke, she realized he was trying to suppress a laugh. She nudged him with her elbow. "Shh ... Nathan doesn't seem to find it funny." Indeed, Nathan looked madder than a hornet's nest, though his mate seemed to be doing a good job of calming him down and stopping him from going after them.

"Another one bites the dust," Luke said with a shake of his head. "I just never saw it coming."

"Who is that guy?"

"That's—"

"Mommy! Mommy!"

They both turned their heads to the south side of the street. Grayson practically flew out from Catherine's car and ran at them full speed. She caught him with a short "oomph" as she got the wind knocked out of her. Luke placed his hands on her shoulders to steady her.

"Grayson! I'm so glad you're all right," she said, squeezing him tight and kissing his forehead.

Grayson wrapped his arms around her neck. "Mommy, I did what you said. I found the firehouse and told them to call Chief Will Mason."

"You did good, sweetie. You were so brave and strong."

"I was scared, Mommy," he said with a hiccup. "I thought they were going to catch me. And that I wouldn't ever see you again."

"I'm here," she said, pulling him tight. "And I'm never going to be apart from you again."

"Are we … safe? From the bad men."

Luke placed a hand on Grayson's shoulder. "You are now. I'm never going to let any bad men get to you or your mom. I promise you, Grayson."

"I'm glad you're safe, Luke," Grayson said, rubbing his cheek on his hand.

"I thought for sure those men with the guns …." Georgina felt her throat close up with emotion. "If that dragon hadn't come and saved you …."

Luke's head snapped up abruptly, then looked toward the other end of the street. An older man was in the spot where the dragon stood, amidst the dying flames and the scattered ash. He was down on one knee, his body heaving as he caught his breath.

"Hank!" A woman's shout rang through the air. She ran to him, clothes clutched against her chest. When she held out the clothes to him, he caught her arm instead and pulled her in for a kiss.

Luke tensed visibly, and Georgina guessed who they were. This was Hank and Riva. He was the dragon who saved him. She didn't have to look at his face to know how he was feeling. She just knew.

She nodded at Hank and Riva. "Do you want to see if they're all right?"

His jaw tensed, but he didn't move.

Grayson looked at his mother, and then at Luke. "Luke? Are you okay?"

"I'm fine, Grayson."

The boy wiggled out of his mother's arms and then

grabbed Luke's hand. "It's okay if you're scared of the dragon. I'll be here."

Georgina's heart warmed, and she slipped her hand into Luke's, threading their fingers together. She nudged him. "So will I."

CHAPTER SIXTEEN

Luke swallowed the growing lump in his throat, hoping it would go away. Not that it did any good because the lump went straight to his stomach, weighing it down.

"C'mon," Georgina whispered. "Let's go."

He looked down, first at their hands linked together and then at Grayson's tucked into his other palm. He knew he had to do this. If he was going to move on with his life and be a good mate to Georgina and, possibly, a father to Grayson, he had to let go of the baggage weighing him down. He owed them that much.

With a deep breath, he began to walk. One foot in front of the other with Georgina and Grayson by his side. His chest tightened with each step.

As they drew closer, Riva must have sensed their presence, as she turned her head to face them, her gaze immediately going straight to their linked hands. She gave him a tight smile.

"Luke," she began. "I'm so happy you're safe."

How had he never noticed how tense she was around him

or how her smile never quite reached her eyes? Or maybe he did but was too selfish to care. He let go of Georgina and Grayson and stepped closer to Hank and Riva.

"Are you all right, Luke?" she asked, looking up at him with genuine concern. "You're not hurt are you?" Beside her, Hank merely continued to stare at him, suspicion in his silvery eyes, but he didn't say a word.

"I need to tell you something," Luke began, his throat suddenly closing up.

Her brows knitted together. "You can tell me anything, Luke." She reached up to him with a cautious hand. He grabbed it and wrapped it in his.

"I need to say sorry." That was easier than he thought. He took a deep breath and looked straight into Riva's eyes. "I'm sorry. For what I said that night. For hurting you and tearing our family apart. I said it because I didn't think I was worthy of you after I tried to hurt Hank. I didn't deserve to call you Mom and Dad." He glanced over at Hank, who now looked stunned. "And I know I still don't. I don't care if it takes me a million years, but if you'd let me try, I'd like to earn back that privilege."

Riva opened her mouth, but only a soft cry came out. She stepped forward, wound her arms around him, and squeezed. As sobs wracked her body, he found himself embracing her back.

Hank stepped closer to them and placed one hand on his mate's back and the other on Luke's shoulder. "Son, you never lost it."

Luke couldn't quite describe the feeling those words and his mother's embrace had on him. It was like the anger inside him just dissipated. Still, he knew he had a lot of work to do to make up for years of pushing them away. For now, as they stood still, Luke was content to simply enjoy his mother's arms around him and his father's strong hand on his shoulders.

When Riva finally pulled away, she wiped the tears from her cheeks and looked up at him with a smile—one that made her brown eyes light up. "So," she glanced behind him, "anything you want to tell us?"

Luke turned his head. Georgina was standing there, beaming at him with tears in her eyes. He cocked his head at her, and she nodded, smoothing her hands over her hair and down her shirt as she and Grayson walked closer.

"Ri—Mom, Dad," he said, placing an arm around Georgina, "this is my mate, Georgina Mills, and her son Grayson."

"H-how do you do?" Georgina stammered.

Riva's smile widened. "Georgina, it's lovely to finally meet you." Instead of holding her hand out, she opened her arms and brought her in for an embrace.

Hank, meanwhile, bent down to Grayson's level. "Hi Grayson, it's nice to meet you."

Grayson stayed behind her and kept his face hidden, but Georgina nudged him. "Say hi, sweetie. He's Luke's dad."

That seemed to alleviate his shyness and he slowly moved toward Hank.

Hank gave him a warm smile. "Thank you for helping everyone in Blackstone. You saved the entire town."

His mouth hung open. "I did?"

Hank nodded. "You did. I heard you were very brave, escaping from the bad men and coming here to warn us about the bombs."

He looked up at his mother. "Mommy said I could do it. She believed in me."

Riva, who had bent down next to her husband, looked up

at Luke warmly. "Yes, mommies tend to do that." She turned back to Grayson. "Hello, Grayson."

"Say hi to Miss Riva," Georgina urged.

"Hello, Miss Riva," he said.

Riva grinned. "Please. Call me Grams."

As more and more people arrived on Main Street, Hank shuffled them to the sidewalk to allow the emergency crews to start working. Police Chief Meacham told them they had rounded up all of The Organization's hired goons and were taking them to the station. Christina also said her brothers were taking care of all the bombs and diffusing them for real.

"We should see if anyone else needs help," Hank said to his wife, then turned to Luke. "Why don't you come to the castle tonight? I'm sure we could all use some time to unwind and celebrate, after today. We'll have everyone over."

"That sounds great," Luke said.

"We'll see you later, then, Luke, Georgina, Grayson," Riva said before Hank led her away.

Luke bent down and picked up Grayson with one arm, then put his other arm around Georgina. He pulled them close, his lion roaring in happiness as he held the two most important people in the world.

EPILOGUE

GEORGINA SHUT down her computer and stretched her arms overhead. *Another work day done.* She was glad to finally be headed home. And, to top it all off, it was Friday. She wanted nothing more than to spend every minute of Saturday and Sunday with Luke and Grayson. Maybe they could have brunch at Rosie's and then catch a movie in the afternoon. Sybil wanted to get together at some point, too. Kate was apparently having some crisis and needed a girl's night. If she could convince Luke to babysit on Saturday evening, she could manage it.

It was hard to believe the attack on Blackstone had been over a week ago. Sure, everyone still seemed guarded and on edge, but for the most part, things had returned to normal. They were still repairing the damage to Main Street, and the road was closed, though a few businesses remained open. Everyone was volunteering to help with repairs, while places like Rosie's, Giorgio's, and the other restaurants were donating food and refreshments. There was talk of a grand re-opening, which would be a celebration of sorts.

The entire town had been swept for bombs and other dangers. Christina, whom Georgina found out was actually the head of the Blackstone Division of the Shifter Protection Agency, said they had gotten rid of all the explosives. She did, however, warn them that this wasn't the end. Though The Chief had been captured and taken away, The Organization was possibly still operating out there. The Blackstone SPA was making it their mission to stamp them out.

The elevator dinged, interrupting her thoughts. She glanced at the clock. It was after six. *Who could it be?* Matthew had left to go to a dinner meeting, while Jason practically lived at the SPA headquarters on the 15th floor with Christina. She wasn't expecting anyone to come, much less this late.

Moments later, Riva and Hank Lennox stepped out, with, much to Georgina's surprise, Grayson between them, his hands tucked into theirs. The older couple had decided to stay in Blackstone for another week or so before continuing with their 'round-the-world' trip. Georgina, Luke, and Grayson spent almost every evening having dinner at Blackstone Castle with them and the whole family. Just last night, they had a goodbye dinner for Nathan and Violet, who were headed back to Eritana to continue with the building of the orphanage.

"Mommy!" Grayson cried, running to her and hugging her legs. "Grams and Pop-pop got me out of daycare!"

"That's nice of them," she said, ruffling his hair. Then, she turned a confused look at Riva and Hank. "I'm so sorry, Luke didn't mention we would be having dinner again or anything. Not that I mind, though Meg's cooking certainly isn't doing anything for my figure," she said with a laugh.

Riva and Hank looked at each other. "Actually—" Riva was

interrupted by the sound of the elevator's arrival. "Ah, looks like I won't have to stall after all."

"Stall?" Georgina asked. When she saw the familiar figure standing in the doorway, it made her even more confused. "Luke?"

Luke was wearing a suit and carrying a large bouquet of roses in one hand. His hair was bound back into a ponytail at the nape of his neck, and his beard was neatly trimmed. She thought Luke looked good in t-shirts and jeans (and nothing at all), but in formal wear, he was even more handsome. He looked polished and sophisticated, but there was still that air of danger around him. His tawny golden eyes were looking straight at her, sending a thrill through her.

"Hello, Georgina."

"Don't you look nice," she said. "What's going on?"

Grayson tugged at her skirt. "I'm going to stay at the castle tonight. Pop-pop said he'd show me how the dragons land and take off from the balcony, then we're going for a ride!"

"I don't want to impose—"

"Grayson could never be an imposition," Riva said. "We love having him." She lowered her voice. "And it'll give you two time alone."

Georgina glanced over at Luke. Though he'd been staying over at their house nearly every night, it had been difficult finding some intimate time, especially with Grayson just down the hallway. They'd had a few quick fumbles in the shower in the mornings while he was asleep, but that was about it.

"Are we having dinner out?" she asked.

Luke gave her a wolfish smile. "Among other things. We should get going."

"Wait!" Grayson walked over to Luke and motioned for him to come down to his level. Luke bent down, and the boy whispered something in his ear. "Thank you, and I will," Luke said with a nod, then stood up. "Okay, now we can go."

She waited for Luke, Grayson, or anyone, really, to provide an explanation, but no one did. With a shrug, she got her purse and followed them as they headed to the elevator.

They got to the parking lot, and she said goodbye to Hank, Riva, and Grayson as Luke led her away.

"Are you going to tell me where we're going?" she asked.

Luke looked ahead. "Nope."

She smiled at him wryly. This was certainly new, but then again, she found she was learning so many things about Luke every single day. Like how patient and kind he was, especially when it came to Grayson. Or how sweet and affectionate he could be. She even joked he was like a big kitty cat, with the way he was always rubbing his nose against her cheek or hair. She thought he would find offense with that, but he just laughed.

They stopped in front of a shiny new navy blue truck, and Luke fished some keys out of his pocket before leading her to the passenger side seat. "New truck?"

"The old one wasn't safe," he said. "Not for you or Grayson."

He helped her up, closed the door, and walked around to the driver's seat. Georgina waved to Jenkins the guard as they drove out of the parking lot.

"Are you hungry?" he asked. "It's going to be a long drive."

"No, I'm good, but really, where are we going?"

"It's a surprise," was all he said.

At first, she thought they might be having dinner at the

French restaurant or Giorgio's, but instead of heading into town, Luke turned the opposite way and headed up into the mountains. This was getting more and more confusing by the minute.

After driving for an hour, Luke turned off the highway and onto a small, rough road. A few minutes later, when they emerged from the thick cover of trees, Georgina gasped at what was in front of them.

The glittering lake in the middle of the mountains was gorgeous. The water was a perfect, clear blue and sparkled as the sun's late afternoon rays hit it, filling the valley with light.

"Where are we?" she asked, as she peered out the window.

"The lake doesn't have a name, but most people call it Blackstone Lake. It's private property, though Lennox has their annual summer picnic here." Luke drove for a few more minutes, then pulled into a paved driveway. Up ahead was a small log cabin.

"Oh. Is this where you live?"

He shook his head. "Nah, my place isn't as fancy as this. This was the site of Lucas Lennox's original cabin. When he won the mountains in a card game, he came here and built his home on this spot, with the help of his cousin Eustace Walker. It had been abandoned for decades, but when Dad started working less, he turned it into a getaway of sorts. He and Uncle James spent a week every summer building it together, just like Lucas and Eustace did. But they never really found the time to come here."

He parked the car and cut the engine, then got out and walked to her side.

"If I had known you were getting dressed up, I would have, too," she said as she took his hand and let him help her down.

"You look beautiful." Instead of letting her get on her feet, he lifted her into his arms, then bent his head and kissed her. Georgina practically melted against him. "I've been waiting to do that all day. And other things."

A shiver went through her at his words. She waited for him to kiss her again, but he set her down. He grabbed her hand and tugged at her. "C'mon. The sun's almost setting."

Georgina followed him toward the cabin, walking around the wraparound porch to the back. The view here was even more amazing, as it overlooked the lake. And to her surprise, there was a table in the middle of the back porch, set up with a white tablecloth, flowers, candles, and fancy silverware.

"What is this?" she asked.

"My surprise. I mean, Meg cooked the dinner and all I have to do is get it out of the kitchen. But first, I need to show you something."

Luke led her to the edge of the porch, to where the dock stretched out into the lake. It really was beautiful here—with the sun setting in the distance, the lake underneath them, and the fresh mountain breeze blowing softly. "Luke, it's—Luke?"

As she turned around, she saw Luke on one knee behind her, something shiny between his fingers. The huge diamond's sparkle was even more brilliant than the lake's clear blue waters.

"Georgina, you're already my mate, but if you would do me the honor of being my wife, too, I promise I'll be the best husband to you and father to Grayson. I will love you both until the last breath leaves my body and even after then."

Her throat constricted at the emotions welling up inside her. She would have been satisfied with just being his mate; this was much more than she could have ever hoped for. "Of course," she managed to say. "Yes, I will marry you!"

Luke slipped the ring on her finger and got to his feet. His hands wrapped around her waist and then pulled her to him. "I love you so much," he whispered.

"Are we really alone out here?" she asked.

"Very," he said.

"Hmm … I don't know about you, but I'm not very hungry."

He didn't need further encouragement, it seemed, as he swept her up off her feet and walked her toward the cabin. Luke moved with such speed, she didn't have time to admire the cabin's interior before being laid down on a soft bed.

"I've been waiting for this for a long time," she admitted, lowering her gaze.

His eyes lit up in amusement. "What, quickies in the shower with Marvel Man toys don't do it for you?"

She tossed a throw pillow at him, which he easily lobbed away. He stepped back, and as his fingers began to unbutton his coat jacket, Georgina held her breath. Luke really was a fine specimen of a man. She couldn't take her eyes off him as he began to undress, revealing his well-muscled chest, powerful tattooed arms, and defined eight-pack abs. He unzipped his pants and shucked them, along with his under-wear, off in one motion. His cock was already rock hard and standing at attention. Her own panties grew wet, just thinking of what was about to happen.

For a large man, he really was very graceful. He crawled over to her, taking her shoes off and tossing them over his shoulder. With a wicked smile, he nuzzled at her ankles, up her legs, and then pushed her skirt over her waist.

She stifled a moan when his tongue licked at the damp fabric of her panties. He yanked them aside and stroked her lips with his tongue, lashing at her core and making her hips buck in urgency. He yanked her panties down and quickly threw them aside. When he plunged his tongue inside her, she dug her hands into his hair and squeezed her thighs around his head.

"Ohhh … Luke!" She was surprised by how fast her orgasm came. He didn't stop, however, and continued to lick at her until her body stopped trembling.

Luke reached under her to undo her skirt and slid it off her body. Shyness suddenly filled her as she lay there in the light, bared to him. All the other times, it had been dark or they were in such a hurry that they never had time to really look at each other's body. Feeling self-conscious, she placed her hand over her stretch marks and the soft flesh of her belly.

"No," he said, pulling her hands away. "Never hide from me."

Her heart clenched, watching him reverently place soft kisses on her stomach. When he was done, he moved higher, unbuttoning her blouse and baring her breasts along the way. His mouth was warm and wet as it closed over one nipple, sucking it deep. She could feel his cock, digging at her hips, smearing his pre-cum over her skin.

"Please, Luke. Love me," she whispered.

He popped the nipple out of his mouth and looked up at her with his fierce golden eyes. "I'm gonna love you all night long, Georgina. And for the rest of our lives."

Luke positioned himself between her legs, spreading her thighs apart. She felt the tip of his cock press at her opening, and she hoped she was wet enough to accommodate him. She held her breath as he pushed inside her, slowly and deliberately, as she tried to relax her body. When he was all the way in, she was finally able to breathe. When he made his first thrust, she cried out his name. Then, he continued, pummeling into her and driving her to the edge of her climax. His fingers snaking between them and stroking her clit sent her over.

He continued, thrusting into her a few more times, then rolled them over until she was on top. He urged her to ride him. Placing her hands on his chest, she began to move her hips, sliding him in and out of her, the friction driving them both wild. They looked in each other's eyes, getting their rhythm together so he would thrust up at the moment she bore down on him. Oh God, yes ... her body was tightening again and ...

"Ohhh!" She fell on top of his chest, bracing herself as her orgasm crashed through her body, her hips seemingly moving on their own as she slid him in and out of her. His arms wrapped around her, gripping her as he continued thrusting. A growl escaped his lips, and she felt his body tense. She wasn't sure if it was their mating bond, but even his orgasms felt intense to her, making her shiver in delight and reveling in the thought that she gave him pleasure. When his breathing evened out, she sighed and relaxed her body as she lay on top of him.

A few minutes later, Luke rolled her over and slipped out of her. He pushed her hair away from her nape and kissed her neck. Sliding his hand over her arm, he moved down so he could entwine their fingers together, the diamond grazing over his palm.

She sighed, then waited a heartbeat before asking, "When should we tell Grayson?"

His chest rumbled in a chuckle. "He already knows."

"What?"

"I asked his permission. Before I planned this whole thing," he said, planting a kiss on her shoulder. "I told him I loved you very much and that I love him, too. And that I wanted all of us to be a family, together."

Her breath hitched. "When we were at the office, what did he whisper to you?"

She felt him smile against her skin. "He said, 'if Mommy says no, you should bribe her with mac and cheese. It works on me.'"

She chuckled and turned to face him. "No need for mac and cheese, though." Reaching up, she touched his cheek, the soft hairs of his beard tickled her palm. "I love you, Luke."

"And I love you, my mate." His strong arms wrapped around her, then pulled her closer to him. As he kissed her, she felt it all over again. The zing, the warmth, and the love flowing from him. They had fought for their love, for their families, and for each other and come out on the other side scarred but intact. As they lay in each other's arms, it was as if all the wrongs in the world, their worries and fears, dissipated into thin air, leaving nothing but peace and clarity.

At this moment, finally, everything in the world felt *right*.

Dear Reader,

YOU ARE CORDIALLY INVITED TO THE WEDDING OF
GEORGINA MILLS
AND
LUCAS LENNOX III

Sign up for my newsletter here:
http://aliciamontgomeryauthor.com/mailing-list/

Of course, you might catch a glimpse of Kate's story.

Though you'll get to read all of it in the next book:

THE BLACKSTONE SHE-WOLF

TURN THE PAGE FOR A PREVIEW AFTER THE AUTHOR'S NOTES

When I first envisioned the Blackstone series, I didn't have much in my head. I knew wanted to write about a town full of shifters, an almost utopia where they could live in peace and harmony. I also knew that there would be dragons (because I wanted to write about dragons) but also other types of shifters.

If you've read The Last Blackstone Dragon, then you know I've been planning Luke's story from the beginning. After Matthew and Jason's story (which were plots brewing in my head for a decade), Luke's was the next story I started thinking about. Since he was going to be the last in this series, I knew I had to plan for it, leaving you little clues throughout the other books to hint at what happened between him and Riva. Their reunion scene was a heart breaking one to write, simply because I'd been envisioning it in my head for so long. I had a good long cry after I wrote it.

At one point I was going to abandon the whole subplot. I love Riva and Hank so much, I just didn't want them to go through the heartbreak. I have another strange reason why I was not going to do it at all, and it has something to do with *Star Wars: The Force Awakens*.

Let me explain (though feel free to skip the next four paragraphs if you're not interested):

I'm a HUGE Star Wars fan. And, being a romantic at heart, in my mind, after Return of the Jedi, Princess Leia and Han Solo lived happily ever after. But they did not, as the movie tells us. And, while I love the new movies, it came at a great cost: we come to find out that there was no happy ever after. I was crushed for a while, but now I've come to terms with it.

So, I didn't want something similar to happen to Hank and Riva. Not that I would ever think of them being apart, but I just didn't want for them to go through a similar heartbreak Han and Leia did (or must have gone through.).

But I realized, this was all part of the journey. Despite wanting them to be, Hank and Riva were not perfect people. They made mistakes, too and while they did the best they can, they had to deal with the consequences.

I hope that I haven't ruined the love story of Hank and Riva for you. For me, the decision was almost like realizing that your parents aren't perfect. When we're young, we look up to them and think they are the world. Unfortunately, we all eventually come to realize that they are only human too.

So, even though I said Luke's was the last story in the Blackstone series, along comes this very loud voice in my head, asking for her story.

Kate.

I can almost hear her in my head now, saying , "Don't break up the band, Alicia!".

And so because I follow my muse and my readers, I'll be

bringing you Kate's, Amelia's, and Sybil's stories in the next months.

Hold on to your seats it's going to be a bumpy ride.

All the best,

Alicia

PREVIEW: THE BLACKSTONE SHE-WOLF

"Motherfucking douche nozzle!" Kate Caldwell cursed as she slammed her palm on her keyboard. She reached over to her side table, grabbed the half-empty can of *POWERJOLTZ* energy drink, and took a healthy swig. Swinging back to face the computer monitor, she took a deep breath and pressed "unmute" on her phone.

"Are you there, Miss Caldwell?"

"I'm here, Mr. Dennis." *You twatwaffle.* She bit her lip so hard to stop herself from saying that out loud it nearly bled. "Now, tell me again what's wrong with the buttons for your app *this time?*"

"Well, I think you need to move them more to the left," Martin Dennis said.

"Uhm, you told me to move them to right the last time," she reminded him.

He ignored her. "And also, the background is too blue."

"But your last email said, and I quote, 'make the background blue-er'."

"Yes, but now it's too blue."

Kate pressed the mute button again and let out a scream. After two seconds, she unmuted the call. "So, a little *less* blue but not *too* blue." This time, she couldn't stop the sarcastic tone in her voice.

Dennis let out an unhappy grunt. "Is there a problem, Miss Caldwell? You know, I could go to another designer who can do this for us."

"No, no problem at all." Her fingers turned into claws and scratched down the leather arm rests of her chair. *Damn wolf.* "I'll get to work."

"Great, great!" he said. "Now, before you go, there are a couple of other things I need to talk about …."

Kate gave a silent groan and glanced at the clock. She really needed to get out of here *now*. As if it wasn't bad enough, the notifications on her personal phone were blowing up as Martin Dennis kept droning on and on about another project they were working on.

She wanted to tear her hair out. But Barkely Industries was one of her best anchor clients, and she needed the money. Sure, if she had taken a full-time job at Lennox Corp. she'd be raking in the dough, but Kate preferred the freedom of being a freelance software engineer and app designer. There was nothing like being her own boss and dictating her own hours, but it was times like this when she dreamt of having a corner office, putting her heels up on her desk, and ordering her minions around.

"… did you get that last thing, Miss Caldwell?" he asked.

"What? Uh, of course Mr. Dennis." What the fuck had he been droning on about? "I really should get off the phone now, so I can make these changes for you."

"Right. I'll expect the changes by morning. Have a good day, Miss Caldwell."

Ugh, she hated how he always called her that. No matter how many times she told him to call her Kate, he insisted on calling her 'Miss Caldwell' in that condescending sneer of his. "You too." *Thundercunt.*

Kate had never been so happy to end a call. The line had barely dropped before she was on her feet, grabbing her phone, jacket, and keys and heading out the door.

Her inner wolf urged her on. It understood the urgency of the events happening in Blackstone.

"I know," she said as she took the stairs two at a time, not bothering to wait for the elevator. With her shifter speed, she made the trip to the garage in less than five minutes. She couldn't waste a single second. Blackstone was in danger, and they needed everyone's hands on deck.

She dashed toward the bright yellow vintage Mustang parked at the end. It was her brother Nathan's car, as was the loft she was currently staying in now. He had given it to her for safe keeping. "No, Kate, I'm not giving her to you," Nathan had said when she asked if she could keep the car. "And you better take care of her!"

Hmmph. As if she couldn't. While she may not have had Nathan or their father's mechanical know-how, she knew how to respect a car, especially a classy piece like the 'Stang. Her dad promised her they'd fix up a car for her too, once him and Ma were back from their retirement trip this year. She couldn't wait as she had already began researching what she wanted. Maybe a Chevelle or a Charger. Electric blue, with a stripe down the middle. She could dye her hair to match, too. But that would have to wait since she needed to pony up the cash first. House sitting for Nathan and Violet helped cut her bills, but she had a long way to go.

For now at least, she could have the pleasure of driving this baby. As she turned the key in the ignition and pressed her foot on the gas, she could hear and feel the power of the engine. The vibrations sent a thrill through her. *Even better than sex*, she thought as she put the car in reverse and backed out of the parking spot.

Not that she'd had any earthshaking experiences lately. When was the last time …? She didn't even want to think about it. Too long. *Does your hooha close up when you don't use it?* Maybe save that one for a Google search later.

She floored it the entire drive, making it to the Lennox Corp. Headquarters in no time, waving at Jenkins the security guard who recognized her and opened the gates as she approached.

As soon as she parked, she whipped her phone out to text Sybil Lennox, her best friend, who was already at Lennox Corp. However, when she heard the flapping of wings and the loud thud as the ground shook, she put the phone away and got out of the car.

A large, twenty-foot dragon had landed in the parking lot, dropping off two figures she recognized as Luke Lennox and —*Thank Jeebus*—little Grayson Mills. From what she'd heard, the bad guys had kidnapped him and his mother. Luke and Sybil must have found him. But where was Georgina Mills? As the dragon flew off, the two dashed through the doors of the main building. Sybil would tell her.

Kate rushed in their direction but slowed down as she got closer to the entrance. As she predicted, seconds later, Sybil Lennox walked around from behind the Lennox Headquarters building, buttoning up her blouse.

"Where have you been?" Sybil admonished as her silvery gray eyes landed on Kate. "I've been texting and calling all morning!"

"I know, I know!" She put her hands up. "Mr. Douchenozzle McDickbag kept me on the phone."

"Martin Dennis again?" Sybil asked as they entered the glass doors and walked to the elevators. "What was the matter *this time?*"

Kate rolled her eyes. "What *isn't* the matter? I can't seem to please the guy. I think it's because he wants my contract to go to his son. Some programmer bro who just got out of college." She huffed and watched as the numbers on the elevator display ascended. "Anyway, catch me up to speed."

As they made their way to the fifteenth floor, Sybil explained what had happened after their friend Georgina and her bear cub, Grayson, were kidnapped. The boy was somehow able to escape their captors, and he found a way to get help and get in contact with them. Sybil and her brother Luke had just arrived from picking them up. Georgina, however, was still with the captors.

"Those sons of bitches!" Kate said.

"We'll find her," Sybil reassured her. "We have to."

The elevator halted, signaling their arrival at the secret headquarters of the The Shifter Protection Agency or simply, The Agency. There was a flurry of activity everywhere, and one of the agents pointed them toward the glass office in the corner. When they walked in, Kate realized that everyone was already there. Like, *everyone*, including Mom, Pop, Nathan, and Violet, who had flown in from out of the country. *Shit.*

"Sorry we're late!" Kate rushed in, not waiting for Sybil. "Motherfuckin' client wouldn't let me off the phone. Kept on and on about how he hated the GUI I made. I told him to stick it up his ass and—"

Holy fuck.

It was like she ran into an invisible solid brick wall, the force nearly knocking her back. But it wasn't a wall. No, it was a pair of eyes the color of the sea that seemed to have had her pinned in place. They bore right into her. His handsome face remained passive, but his nostrils flared.

Mine, her wolf whined.

And his wolf. Oh wow. It roared back so wild and strong that it pushed at her like a wave.

"Petros?" Christina Lennox, head of the The Shifter Protection Agency in Blackstone, said. "You were saying?"

He broke his gaze, turning away from her. "Yes. I mean …."

Everyone's attention went back to him as he spoke. And why wouldn't it? This was life and death after all. It was a good thing too, because then she could ogle him without anyone noticing. She couldn't help it. He was so gorgeous, almost *too* gorgeous. His hair was dark as midnight, and his shoulders were broad and wide. The black shirt he wore clung to his well-developed muscles, and whorls of ink snaked out from under the sleeves. The fabric was so tight, she could see the outline of his abs. His olive skin was tanned, and she wondered if he was the same color all over—

"Kate!" Sybil hissed beside her, nudging her. "Are you listening?"

"Huh? Yeah!" Of course she was listening to him. How could she not? That damn accent was sexy, and the vibrations of his low voice sent heat straight to her core.

Mine!

Her wolf said it so loudly this time, she feared he heard it. And it was like he did, because those blue-green eyes flicked back at her. Her own wolf whimpered and turned, raising its hind quarters to—

Stop it, bitch!

Oh no. This couldn't be. This gorgeous, over six feet of hunky deliciousness with the bangin' bod couldn't be her mate.

Mine.

No no no! There was some mistake. They hadn't even been introduced. And she didn't *want* a mate. Her life was fine just the way it was. She did what she wanted, whenever she wanted. Hell, she did *who* she wanted, though at this moment the thought of being with any other man made her mouth turn to dust.

No. Absolutely not.

They would have a serious discussion about this. Maybe he didn't want a mate, either. He was hot; she bet all the girls threw themselves at him. Why would he want to tie himself down?

Mine, her wolf growled.

Bitch.

Yes, they would have a calm, adult discussion. Of course, not right now. Maybe later, when they saved Blackstone and her panties weren't on fire just looking at him, they would both realize they couldn't possibly be mates.

"So," Christina began, "I'll start assigning teams of two to lead volunteers—"

"I'm going with Vi!" Kate announced, stomping over to her brother's mate.

The tiger shifter's light blue eyes widened with surprise. "Me?"

"What?" Nathan groused. "She should be with me."

"You've had her all to yourself for weeks," Kate pointed out.

"But—"

"Shush!" She looped her arm through Violet's. "It's settled."

The moment Christina finished her briefing with everyone, Kate practically dragged Violet out of the office.

"So," Violet began, "how is everything?"

"Good," Kate said, glancing around them. "I mean, you know, aside from the whole 'our enemies planted bombs all over the place to kill us all' thing. And you? How are the orphans? Anything new?"

Violet gave her a knowing smile. "The girls are healthy and happy. And as for something new," she lowered her voice, "I'm pregnant."

"What?" Kate stopped in her tracks. "Oh my God! Who else knows?"

"Just your mother and father. They were planning to visit us next week with my parents, but we had to tell them as soon as we got here," Violet said.

"Oh my God!" She wrapped Violet in a tight hug. "I'm so happy for you guys! I'm going to be an Auntie!"

"Yes, happy news, for sure." Violet rubbed her stomach. "And well, maybe a cousin to follow soon for my little one?"

"Huh?" Kate feigned. "You know what? I think it doesn't make sense for us to be partners—" She tried to turn and get away, but Violet's grip on her arm was too strong, plus Kate would never push a pregnant broad.

"That wolf is your mate."

"Who?"

The tiger shifter crossed her arms over her chest. "You know who. The big, surly-looking guy. I know the look that passed between you two."

Damn. Violet was too smart for her own good. "It's not what you think," Kate said. "I don't even know him. We might not be compatible."

"Well, then, you'll have to get to know him. Don't tell Nathan I said so, but that Greek wolf is hot."

"Greek?"

"Yes, he's from Lykos."

"Oh." So he came here with Ari Stavros all the way from Greece. Which meant he wouldn't be staying too long. She convinced herself that was for the best.

"Speaking of which." Violet nodded her head to the left.

Kate turned her gaze down the hall and swallowed a big lump in her throat. The Greek wolf was stalking toward them, his large body tense as he walked with slow, lumbering steps. She found herself paralyzed by his gaze again, and it was only when Violet kicked her shin that she was able to move her limbs. By this time, he was already inches away from her. He raised an arm toward her.

"You are—"

"Sorry, gotta go!" Kate said, ducking under his massive bicep. "I think I hear Sybil calling me!" She waved as she dashed down the hallway.

She turned the corner, listening for footsteps behind her, but it seemed he didn't follow her. Placing a hand over her hammering heart, she calmed herself. *Okay*, she thought, *all I have to do is avoid him until he leaves.* Or, rather, first, save the town while avoiding him. *Easy peasy.* She was a master at avoiding responsibility all her life; she could escape one wolf for a few hours.

"Oh God," Kate exclaimed as she watched Uncle Hank transform from a giant fire-breathing dragon into his human form. "We did it."

Blackstone was saved. Thanks to the people who stayed behind to look for the bombs planted by The Organization, they were able to find all the explosives and disable their remote detonation devices. The Chief, their leader, tried to set them off manually, but Luke and Uncle Hank had stopped them.

Relief swept through her, and as the adrenaline left her body, her shoulders sagged. She had spent the last few hours combing every inch of her assigned quadrant for bombs with her partner, Kendra Johnson, a female officer from Blackstone P.D. They found two right behind Rosie's Cafe and Bakeshop and had quickly called it in so they could be diffused. They were guarding the bombs, making sure none of the goons from The Organization could get to them, when they heard the sound of gunshots coming from Main Street.

Kate ran out and saw everything—how Uncle Hank had swooped down to protect Luke with his bulletproof body. When fire and lava spewed from his mouth, the heat was nearly unbearable, and Kate covered her face with her arm.

But now, it was over. And everything would be fine. Oh, and it looked like Luke and Georgina were reuniting. They were embracing and—

"You have been avoiding me."

Oh crap.

Slowly, she pivoted on her heel. "I wouldn't call it avoiding as much as, uh, giving us some space."

Ocean-colored eyes stared down at her. "I do not need any space from you, *mate.*"

"Wait!" She raised her hands as he approached her.

He stopped. "Yes?"

"Well, I—oh look over there! I think there's a bomb!" She pointed behind him, and he turned his head. While he was distracted, she took her chance and made a mad dash for the opposite direction.

Ha! That stu—"Hey! What the fuck?"

The entire world turned upside down. Oh no, wait, it wasn't the world. It was her. That cocky bastard had her over his shoulder and was now carrying her away to God knows where.

"Put me down, you—you—*caveman!*" she screamed at him. "What the hell do you think you're doing?" She kicked her legs and beat her fists down his broad back, but he didn't even flinch.

All her blood rushed to her head, and she lost all sense of thought. Yeah, that was probably why she was staring at his ass instead of trying to fight him off. And oh *fucking hell*, he smelled good. Hmmm … like the sea, clean and fresh with just a hint of sweat. Her wolf was going crazy, urging her to touch him.

She yelped when he finally put her upright. Where the hell were they? Glancing around, she saw they were in the empty parking lot behind the bookshop on Main Street. The blood draining out of her head made her dizzy, and she stepped back, bracing herself against the solid wall behind her.

"Are you all right?" he asked, his voice suddenly gentle.

"I'm fine!" she said. "No thanks to you. How could you do that? Carrying me off like some troglodyte?"

"A what?"

"You know. Caveman. Sticks and rocks. Fire. Cave paintings."

He gave her a puzzled look. "English is not my first language, but I will take note and Google it later."

"Yeah, you do that." She tried to turn away from him, but he placed his arm across her, planting his palm on the wall to stop her.

"You are my mate," he said. "You must have felt it. Heard our wolves call to each other. I've searched for so long … I thought I would never find you. You're more exquisite than I could have imagined."

His words sent a shiver through her, and her knees wobbled like jelly. He thought she was exquisite? She couldn't remember any man ever saying that to her. Maybe hot. And sexy. And that they liked her small tits. But not *exquisite*, like she was something to be worshipped and cherished forever, not just for a couple hours of fun.

No! This wasn't right! This wasn't how it was supposed to be. This was too much. "Look, uh, what's your name again?"

"Petros Thalassa."

"Right. Petros." She put a hand on his chest. Jeez, it was like a rock. "This isn't how we do things in America."

"I know, but you wouldn't—"

"Look, I don't believe in mates."

"You do not?"

She shook her head. "I believe in choices. I'm a modern woman, you know? And I believe we should have a choice in who we spend the rest of our lives with, or if we even choose to do that at all."

His jaw set. "I would never force myself on you."

"What? Oh, I'm not talking about *that*." Of course, her dirty, dirty mind immediately went to *that*, and she was pretty sure there wouldn't be any need for force. "Look, I'm sure you're a great guy, Petros. I'm just not looking for anyone right now, ya know? My life is fine the way it is."

"But we are mates," he said. "Fated to be together, me and you ... uh ..." His brows knitted together.

"Kate," she supplied, rolling her eyes.

"Kate." He gave a nod. "A beautiful name. Like you."

"Uh, thanks?"

He reached down and wrapped his large hands around her wrists, the touch sending a zing of electricity across her skin. "Kate-mine, you are a worthy mate," he said. "And you will be a strong mother to our pups—"

"Just hold on a minute!" she cried, struggling to raise her hands. "Did you not understand a single word I said? About not looking for anyone right now?"

He nodded. "Of course you are not looking for anyone. I am already here."

"That's not—"

But she didn't get a chance to finish her sentence as he pulled her to him and his lips landed on hers.

Holy. Mother. Of. God.

When she was sixteen, Kate once picked up one of those trashy romance novels Sybil used to read and was so bored by the descriptions that she threw it away. It sounded trite. Trumpets and angels singing in the background? Shivers down the spine? Feeling breathless? It sounded like a load of bull crap, and no boy she ever kissed before that and since then made her feel that way.

But this *kiss*? Oh fuck.

Petros' lips were warm against hers, rough and demanding, coaxing her to respond. Kate realized he let go of her wrists, so she wound her arms around his neck to pull him down closer. His body slammed against hers, pushing her up against the wall and trapping her there. That fucking amazing tongue of his snaked inside her mouth, tangling with her own. He tasted like the sun and the ocean and the earth ... she couldn't describe it, but that was the closest thing she could think of. Inside her, her wolf howled in delight.

Hands moved down from her waist, over her ass, and under her knees. He lifted her up and wrapped her legs around his waist. Fucking hell, she could feel the significant bulge of his cock rubbing right against her. Right *there*. Her panties were soaked through in an instant. He was perfectly lined up against the seam of her pussy, like he knew just how to position his body to send tingles of pleasure all over her. Oh God, she was going to come, right out here in the open, riding Petros as he continued to rub himself on her.

"Ahem."

They both froze, and while Kate's arms fell down to her side, Petros didn't move and kept her pinned against the wall.

"I hate to interrupt ... whatever this is," Jason Lennox said in a wry voice. "But we've still got work to do."

Petros cleared his throat, unwound her legs from his waist, then set her down. He turned around. "Of course. Apologies. We were carried away."

"From what I heard, you were the one doing the carrying away." Jason looked at Kate. "Kate, are you ... okay? Do you need me to—"

Petros stepped in front of her. "Of course she is okay. She is my mate."

"Oh." Jason sounded relieved. "Well, I guess I can tell Christina to give you five more minutes."

"Wait!" Kate called, but Jason was already gone. She looked at Petros and then smacked him on the arm. *Ouch, that hurt.* "Why did you say that to him?"

"Because it is the truth."

"But that's not ... you can't ... that's not the point!" She let out a frustrated sound.

"What does it matter? Soon everyone will know," he said matter-of-factly.

"Arggh!" She stamped her foot in irritation. "You stubborn wolf! Why won't you listen to me?"

He placed a hand on her shoulder. "Kate-mine, I am listening to you. To your wolf. It wants me as much as you do."

"Gah!" she choked in anger. She wanted to deny it, but for some reason she couldn't make the words come out of her mouth. "I can't do this! You ... you stay away from me! Go back to Lykos!"

"But—"

She waved a hand at him. "I swear to God, you come near me and you'll regret it!"

Petros' face turned stormy, but he nodded. "I will leave you be for now. Perhaps you need some time to come to your senses." He turned those intense blue-green eyes back at her. "But know this: you cannot stop fate."

She stared after him as he walked away. The wind whooshed right out of her lungs, and it was hard to breathe. His words rang in her head. They sounded like a promise. No, they were a threat.

Oh yeah? Well, she didn't do well when she was threatened. *I'll show you, asshole.* Oh no, she was not going to just bend over to fate. She would fight it kicking and screaming.

Available now on Amazon!

Made in the USA
Las Vegas, NV
27 November 2023